D1547383

IMAGO
and Other Transformations

Erica Ruppert

TREPIDATIO
PUBLISHING

ISBN: 978-1-68510-086-5 (sc)
ISBN: 978-1-68510-087-2 (ebook)
Library of Congress Catalog Number: 2022951372

First printing edition: March 17, 2023
Published by Trepidatio Publishing in the United States of America.
Edited by Sean Leonard
Proofreading, Interior Layout, and Cover Layout by Scarlett R. Algee
Cover Artwork and Design by Don Noble

Trepidatio Publishing, an imprint of JournalStone Publishing
3205 Sassafras Trail
Carbondale, Illinois 62901

Trepidatio books may be ordered through booksellers or by contacting:
JournalStone | www.journalstone.com

To my mother, who should have been a writer

Contents

III. Gods and Monsters

Publication History

About the Author

IMAGO
and Other Transformations

I. Lost Souls

Fracture

TESS'S SKIN GROWS suddenly cold and slick with sweat. She is suspended in space, her limbs not her own to command, and blurred grey figures move at the edge of her vision. She cannot see directly before her. She cannot feel the chair beneath her. The book of incantations she read from falls from her lap. The spell seizes her, stronger than flesh. At a distance she hears her own voice spewing a garbled monologue.

Other voices override her.

"What happened? Is she all right?"

"Lay her down!"

She is dragged onto the ground. She cannot steer her body. Words are locked in her head, the pattern unravelling. Her mouth spasms. She speaks in tongues. Someone pulls her limbs straight. Her muscles resist. It feels like falling. There is something else with her, riding her. It is not what she called.

"Is she having a seizure?"

"She's not breathing! Call 911!"

She has no memory after that.

#

She wakes in a sterile room. Light fills the open window above her bed. She breathes in the sharp air deeply. It makes her sneeze.

She kneels and leans out the window. Winter, the whole world crystal. The light hurts her eyes and she sits back down. The bed she is in is wide and soft, white as a cloud. She lies back in the smothering pillows and goes back to sleep.

A needle-prick, bright as broken glass. She opens her eyes. The room is plush in shadows. A woman bends over her, empty syringe raised away.

"Oh, you're with us," the woman says.

Tess raises her hand through empty space, brushes the woman's cheek with dry fingers. She recognizes her, but can't place from where.

"Am I alive?" she says, her voice rough.

The woman smiles at her, suspended in dusk.

"Of course you are."

But the woman is not. Tess sees past the smile into darkness, and screams.

Someone strides into the room, hitting switches to unleash the glare of overhead fluorescents. The revenant dissolves like a stain in the light.

Tess cannot focus. She hears the clatter of activity in the corridor, voices, machinery, the dull click of footsteps. She comes back to herself with a shock.

The nurse feels her forehead, takes her pulse, speaks at her with quick reassurance.

Her eyes lock onto the nurse's face. It is plain, and real.

She holds onto that. The nurse strokes hair back from Tess's face like she is petting a dog.

"You'll be okay."

Tess nods from the deep pillow. The nurse leaves her with the door ajar. The window above her is shut tight. Heat rising from the radiator stirs the curtains. She watches them, wondering at the invisible currents in the air.

When Tony comes in, she stumbles up to greet him. He catches her before she can fall.

"I want to go home," she says.

"All right," Tony says. His eyes shine.

He guides her out of the hospital into the cold glassy night. The air sparkles with ice fragments. She huddles against him.

It is warm in the car. The streets are quiet. The tires hiss on the wet pavement. Tony rubs her neck the way she likes it. She gazes serenely out the window until the city shimmers like dust drifting in the light, unstill, impermanent. She blinks and turns away. She does not trust her eyes, closes them until the car stops and they are home.

As they climb the narrow stairs, the noise of a crowd spills out through the open door. Golden light washes over them like firelight. She is surprised to see so many people in the tiny apartment. She recognizes some of them, but other faces are merely place-holders, as if balloons were used to fill the empty spots.

She freezes on the threshold. The spellbook still lies on the floor where it fell. Black dust sifts from its pages, all its patterns unmade. Tony urges her into the warmth.

"You're back," someone says, embracing her. Tess twitches at the words. She turns to see the revenant, close as the breath she draws to scream. Bands of light and darkness crackle across her field of vision like stuttering film. She cannot feel the arms around her. She cannot feel the floor. She tries to turn, slipping sideways. Colors smear. Tony pulls at her. She reels.

The room is silent. Waiting.

She looks around her, searching for an anchor.

"Tony?"

He touches her temples lightly. Static spits from her skin.

"It followed you back. It will follow again."

She digs her knuckles hard into her eyes. Stars burst there and fade away.

"Where?" she says.

There is no answer.

She looks past his calm face, past the darkness. He isn't there. He never was. The light beyond him is blinding. She steps through him into the glaring white. Nothing follows.

The Bones

THE BONES LAY like a mosaic on the damp dirt floor, so old they no longer smelled of death. Toni had no idea how they had gone undisturbed so long. The debris in the basement's corners spoke of other break-ins, other explorations. She kicked crushed cans out of her way as she made her way closer to the bare brown skeleton. A faint thrill of fear fluttered under her heart, but it was distant. She had sought it out so often that it had dulled.

Light from the high broken windows reached into the room like a mist. Toni played her flashlight beam over the curved ribs, fleshing them out with their own shadows. The skeleton was on its back, looking as if it had fallen there. It looked complete, from what Toni could tell.

Between the long fragile bones of the skeleton's hand stood a flat rectangle the size of a postcard. Toni reached for it gingerly, pinching a corner between her fingers. It was an old sandwich bag folded over on itself, and it tore as she lifted it free. What the decayed plastic protected was still intact.

She moved closer to the windows to let the thin sunlight drift over her shoulder. The filthy plastic crumbled as she opened it. She let the tatters drop and unfolded the brittle paper inside.

The pencil drawing had blurred as the paper aged, but it was still a recognizable portrait. Toni glanced over the paper's edge to the skeleton sprawled at the edge of the light. The angle was right, the skull's tilt, the bend of the leg. On the paper, a woman's breasts lolled, her hair spread out across the dirt, her eyes shut as in sleep. Whoever had drawn this had included the bruises around her throat.

Now Toni felt the fear as more than the weak beating of wings in her throat. She shifted her feet, felt grit roll under her soles. Now. Here. This was where the artist had stood. She looked back down at the paper. The woman had been pretty enough, her nose a little pugged but a sweet face.

She folded the paper carefully along its old creases and slid it into her back pocket. Then she hitched herself out through the broken window she had used to get in.

The street was quiet, even for this early in the day. The neighborhood was fading out slowly, its inhabitants shifting further east in the city. Too many of these buildings were empty now, except for the squatters. Toni walked the two blocks back to her car. She'd left it parked in a neighborhood where people still lived.

Her hand left a smear of blood where she gripped the wheel. She'd cut it getting out of the basement, she thought. Cocooned in her car, the fear she dragged out with her eased. She realized she had forgotten to take any pictures of the body, of the lonely cellar, of the garbage.

As she drove out she thought the streets seemed emptier than they had when she had come in. She headed back over the highway to familiar territory.

#

At home she opened up the drawing again, smoothed it out gently and pinned it to the board above her desk. The paper had taken on a pale ivory tint from age. Toni stared at it for long minutes, memorizing the smudged pencil shadows of the woman's face, the dark pool of her hair, the curve of her thighs. The detail in the drawing gave her a strange impression, as if the artist had traced over a photograph to make this.

She took the drawing down long enough to scan it and open it with the freeware modeling program she had downloaded. Her shoulders already tight, she leaned in to her screen and got to work.

Willa came in with a clatter of keys as she dropped them on the entryway table. She was never quiet. Toni's eyes flickered to her and then back to the screen.

"So, did you find some inspiration?" Willa said.

"Yeah," Toni said. Her hand hovered over the mouse as she studied what she had done so far. "Up on the other side of the Forty-Three. The neighborhood up there is emptying out."

Willa walked past Toni and into the kitchen. She opened the refrigerator, closed it again. A drawer clattered open. Silverware clicked. Toni shut her eyes, wishing the distractions away.

"Everyone's moving away from that end of town," Willa said, loud enough to be heard across the apartment. "I hear it's not safe up there anymore."

"I know," Toni said, pressing her fingers to her temples. "It's pretty creepy with hardly anyone around."

Willa came back into the living room with a sandwich in her hand. Toni opened her eyes to refocus on the screen.

"Look, Toni," Willa said. "Let me go up there with you if you go again. Safety in numbers and all that."

"All right," Toni said, not turning around. "Now I gotta work."

Willa came up behind her and leaned over her shoulder to look. Toni tensed at the intrusion. At first Willa said nothing, only breathed into Toni's hair.

"Well," she said after a moment. "That's a pretty messed-up self-portrait you've got going on."

Toni brushed her away.

"Shut up. It's a drawing I found today."

"Where was it? It looks like you. Or is that what you're trying to do?"

Toni didn't answer.

#

It was closer to morning than night when Toni finally shut down and went to bed.

The night outside the window was too quiet, without even a distant rumble of traffic. Toni curved herself around Willa's warm back for comfort and reached up to stroke her face. Her hair had fallen over it, and Toni brushed it away. Willa's hair felt thick and wavy under her hands, and the curls tangled in her fingers. Toni pulled her hand away. That wasn't Willa's hair. Who she held didn't smell like Willa, was too tall and too muscular. Toni screamed in the dark, awake.

The bedsheets fell in a tidal wave as Willa threw them up and back and rolled to grab at Toni's shoulders, shaking her out of nightmare. In the dim glint of streetlights through the window, Toni could see it was the right Willa. Toni stopped screaming and clutched at her, still caught between.

#

Over the next few days Toni built up the face in clay, copying the model she had made of the sketch. She pressed her thumbs into the soft clay, smoothing out the curve of the cheeks, the pinch of the chin, the wide-set eyes.

It looked like the drawing and her 3D model of the drawing. But any initial sweetness Toni had seen in the face was gone. It was still pretty, and recognizable from the pencil sketch. But Toni didn't like looking at it anymore. There was a cast to it now that cooled her blood.

She took a picture of her sculpture before she mashed the clay back into a featureless mass and rewrapped it in plastic bags for storage. She didn't want to see it any longer, not as a physical presence in her world. The woman's sketched features already followed her, living through her eyes.

Toni imagined the woman in many faces now, reflected in windows, caught in profile in a moving crowd of pedestrians, in the background of videos. One morning Toni thought she saw the woman turn the corner in her hallway just as she stepped out of her apartment. Toni took to staying in more than she went out. She worked on the computer model she had made, changing the angles, altering the features, trying to find something familiar in it. It looked more and more like her as she tweaked it. She didn't dare erase it. It had gone too far.

#

Toni thought she could perform an exorcism of sorts if she went back, if she returned the pencil sketch to its keeper. Maybe if she stood the folded drawing back between those dry fingers she would be rid of its power over her imagination. She knew it was magical thinking. She didn't care.

She parked on the block she had used the first time, but now even this area was becoming depopulated. At this rate, she and Willa would need to start looking for a new place soon. She walked quickly, head down, hands clenched in her jacket pockets, waiting for a threat that didn't come. She had trouble finding the building again. It seemed as if the neighborhood had fallen to ruin in the few weeks since she had found it. The street sign was down, and more than one apartment house on the block had burned and fallen and left a jagged gap behind.

She walked up and down the block, aware of how alone she was. Finally, one shabby building seemed familiar, and Toni thought she recognized the unbarred broken window she had used before. She bent low to peer into darkness, holding her phone up for its fragile light. Shadows hung in the air like a haze of smoke. There were shapes on the floor that might be a narrow figure, a sheen that could be long, bare teeth. Toni wriggled down and put her head through the window. She thought something moved in the depths of the room, scratching the floor. It could have been her own shadow, her own sounds. She could not be sure. She stood free of the window, quickly, her heart beating fast.

Every window was an empty eye on her. Toni wished she had parked closer. She drew her shoulders up against the solitude and walked to her car without looking back.

#

Toni stared when Willa pulled open the apartment door for her before she could turn the key. She thought Willa would still be at work. Toni walked past her with a scant shrug and started her laptop. Behind her she heard the door click shut, light footsteps, the creak of furniture. Toni tried to keep her eyes on the screen, but Willa coughed for attention. Toni turned half-around, just enough to see her.

"Where did you get to today?" Willa asked, lounging in a sloppy heap on the sprung sofa.

"Other side of the Forty-Three."

She swung back to her laptop. Toni knew better than to open up the modeling program and look at that face again, but she still did. Willa sighed behind her, getting up.

"I wish you'd have let me know."

Toni saved the project and logged off. She couldn't gauge how upset Willa was. "I wasn't sure I could find it again."

"Did you?"

Willa stood over her. Toni looked up. "Yes."

"And?"

Willa's face shifted as uncast shadows moved across it. Toni blinked and rubbed at her eyes. She turned away.

"It was empty. Just empty."

#

Toni spent the night in the living room, lonely from Willa's anger. She set her alarm for too early, hoping to escape the apartment's confines before

Willa woke. But the silence of the building around her kept her restless and half-awake, waiting for some human sound to come. The emptiness had followed her back. Shadows coiled through the lace curtains like strands of hair, and she dreamed the face behind them.

Toni finally stopped dreaming with the morning, and slept through the alarm's bright buzz. When she got up Willa was in the kitchen, and it was too late to leave without a fight. She didn't have the energy for it. She tried to walk out before it could happen.

"Where are you going?" Willa asked, stopping her at the door.

Toni looked away. Willa stood her ground. She took Toni's chin in her hand and made her look at her.

"You have someone."

Toni pulled her head free. "Don't be stupid."

"I'm coming with you," Willa said. Toni squirmed like an embarrassed teen.

"I'll wait for you downstairs," Toni said then, guilty and impatient, and she headed down the hall to the elevator while Willa was finding her shoes.

Toni walked out of the building and saw that the desolation had come to her. The steps of their building were cracked, the façade caked with graffiti. The only cars on the street were stripped-out shells. The one in front of her building still had faded memorial poppies hanging from the rearview mirror. She realized it was hers.

Willa should have been right behind her. Toni turned, frightened.

"Willa?" she called. Her voice fell flat in the empty street. She turned back, up the steps and back through the peeling door.

"Willa? Where are you?"

The foyer was filthy, littered like an animal's den. Had it been like that when she came down? Toni couldn't remember. The elevator door was jammed halfway open now. She was sure it was working a minute ago.

She noticed that the basement door was chocked open. It was never left open. That was one of the superintendent's pet peeves, and he enforced it. She peered into the shadows of the ugly stairwell. "Willa!" she called again. A voice came back to her. She wasn't sure it wasn't her own. Wishing for stronger light, Toni started down.

The same decay in the streets had ruined the basement. The elevator doors were blocked with old furniture. The storage lockers were opened and looted. Hook-ups from the washers and dryers dangled against the unfinished brick wall, the machines gone. Toni remembered a tiled floor down here, but now there was nothing but dirt.

Pale light came in through the narrow windows at the front of the building. Toni turned toward them. She walked forward, gauging the lay of the room. She knew where she was. Then her feet tangled in the ribcage hidden by shadows and she stuttered in place, fighting gravity and trying not to break the fragile bones with her clumsy feet. She found her balance, bent and moved the bones away. It felt wrong to disturb them after they had lain so patiently for so long. Under her fingers the long ribs were smooth and warm.

Toni looked down at what her hands did, disturbed by the sensation of heat. Her hands were empty, her fingers closed on air. She squatted at the edge of the light, where the bones should be. They were gone, and she crouched in a swept-clean circle on the hard dirt floor.

She stood and looked around her for evidence of the body. There was nothing. She walked to the broken window. There was blood on the frame where she had cut herself getting out. She turned around, recreating her first sight of the dry brown bones. Shadows bent into familiar, suggestive shapes, but the hard skeleton was gone.

Toni walked slowly back to where it had been, where it should have been. She tilted her head, at certain angles catching the distant curve of the skull and the web of the tapering finger bones. The dim light tricked her eyes. The ground beneath her seemed to ripple and fade. She knelt down, feeling heat beneath her knees. It was beneath her. Waiting.

She dug into the packed dirt with a broken chunk of brick, scraping up the hard surface enough to get her fingers into it. She felt her nails tear as she dug, but the pain didn't matter. The hole grew. A hand's-span down, her fingers scraped on something smooth and hollow. When she pried it loose, she saw it was a small plastic box, faded into a milky pink from its long burial. The brittle catch snapped off as she opened it.

Blood smeared the box as she lifted a dull pencil out. Beneath it was a washed-out photograph, curled from being pressed into the narrow box. Toni held it up to the light. It was the woman from the drawing. In the square image she stood in front of the basement window with a pad in the crook of her arm. Her dark hair hung over her shoulders. She was looking down and smiling.

Toni turned on her knees to face the empty window. The picture had been taken from where she crouched now. Where the body lay in the drawing. Her scalp prickled with sudden sweat. Behind her, where the light didn't reach, lead scratched on paper. Sketching her.

Pretty in the Dark

THEIR FIRST NIGHT in camp the wind was up, and Syl heard the old dinner bell ring. It sounded as far away as Mars.

No one had rung it on purpose in years.

But for the wind and the muffled tolling, the night was quiet. Mike dozed restlessly beside her in cabin 9's deep bed. As soon as he saw the cabin he had complained about the lack of modern amenities, but Syl didn't care. Syl's family had come here for decades. Tucked into her wallet was a picture of her at five months old, in her grandfather's arms, in front of cabin 6. Over the years she had slept in every cabin on the property, and knew the rise and fall of the land within the camp well enough to run it at night.

She looked up at the wood plank ceiling. She couldn't see it in the dark, but she knew the knots and grain and the faces they hid. It was good to be back at the lodge after so many years away, and to find so much unchanged.

Long Lake Lodge was how Syl thought of Canada. The camp endured in genteel decline on the northeastern shore of Lake Kashwakamak, a deep gouge in the rock of the Ontario highlands, one of the thousands of water-filled scars left behind by the glaciers. Trapped, the Mississippi River fed the lake, the remains of its currents pushing cold water eastward to the dam.

#

The dam was a destination every year.

Syl had rented one of the old metal motorboats when she booked the cabin, and talked Mike into putting on a stained life vest before they set off. Her father had always insisted on the life vests—the lake might be familiar, but that did not make it safe.

Mike volunteered to man the motor, and Syl sat in the prow and pointed the way he should steer. In the final sweep around a shaggy island, Syl leaned forward, waiting to see the low line of the dam with its blue metal framework and yellow warning chain.

"Slow, now," Syl said to him. "Aim for the tree on the left."

Mike cut the engine and used the oars to push them into the undercut shore. Syl clambered out to tie the boat to the birch that leaned over the water, half its roots tangled in air.

While Mike climbed onto land, Syl ran up the metal steps of the dam and onto the platform. From there she could peer through the grate at the point where the lake became a river again.

She called Mike up beside her to look down the path of the stream here, how the water had jostled and carved the great slabs of rock, rolled them and hollowed them and worn them away.

"The water is down," she said. "We can walk the stream bed."

Syl led him down the sharp slope beside the dam and under the heavy cedar branches, and then splashed her way shin-deep into the cold flowing stream. She waded to a dry outcropping and climbed up. He stayed on the bank.

"Come on," she said. "Follow me. We can go most of the way on the big ones."

Trusting that Mike was behind her, she picked her way downstream. She heard him curse as he stepped into the water. After a minute he caught up.

At points they navigated the shallow water, careful of their footing. Where the stream's path bent, a long slab of pitted granite rose like an island and forced the water into a deep channel against the opposite shore. They climbed up. Sapling birch, cardinal flowers, and yellow grasses found rootholds in the island's water-carved rock. The afternoon sun threw shards of light up from the rushing water. Mike stood still, taking pictures of the trees and the sky. Syl squinted as she looked downstream, then kept moving.

She scrambled over the island, easy as a goat. Every few feet she bent to peer at a loose stone, pocketing the ones banded with quartz. The ones she did not take went back exactly as she had found them.

Then she picked up something different from the litter of sticks and dry crayfish claws that filled the hollows. Not a rock. Not a bleached twig. "Mike," she called out. "Come look at this." She held out the slender bone to him as he bent near.

"Is it a fossil?"

"Hardly," Syl said, turning it between her fingers. It was thin as a drinking straw, dry and grey from exposure. "Probably from a raccoon or a beaver. Maybe a rabbit."

The sound of a branch snapping echoed from the wooded shore. Syl's attention turned.

"There are bears sometimes," she said. "Be loud."

She sang a few lines from a show tune, but Mike did not join her.

"I think I'd like to go now," he said.

"The pond isn't much farther."

"I don't want to go to the pond. Come on. I'm tired," he said.

"We'll take the trail back then," she said.

They climbed away from the stream through the ancient cedars to the portage trail. It was rougher than she had thought it would be, unused, untended, and cluttered with fallen trees, broken by steps made of twisted roots and jutting, lichened rocks. Even where it was relatively level, the trail was littered with pine needles and slippery underfoot.

Over their heads the wind caught high in the trees, rushing through without touching the ground. Clouds turned daylight to shadow.

Syl realized she was moving fast, leaving Mike too far behind. As she turned to wait for him, she caught a shape at the corner of her eye, small and slender and dirty pale. It moved, and she looked straight at it to see a girl in a long, yellowed white dress. The girl looked like a toddler but her face was so old, so drawn and jaundiced. The girl opened her mouth without making a sound, brown lips stretching around a red, red tongue.

Syl screamed and fell backward down the slope off the trail. Boulders and scrub kept her from sliding too far on the slick pine needles.

Mike ran to her as quickly as he could on the rough ground. He skidded down off the trail to where Syl had stopped and helped her climb the short distance back up.

"I thought I saw something," Syl said thinly, her breath still catching. She pointed to a rotten birch stump beside the trail. "I thought that was a person."

"Jeez, Syl," Mike said. "You're lucky you didn't fall where there's a real drop."

Syl brushed brown needles and rotten leaves from her hair and clothes. Her palms were scraped and tattooed with black dirt. She felt a knot growing behind her right ear where she'd clipped a rock.

Syl looked down the trail, back the way they'd come. Wind whistled above them.

"Let's go," she said. "I think it's going to rain."

#

When rain came at Long Lake Lodge, the cabins became claustrophobic. Syl talked Mike into going up to the common room in the lodge.

Here, the relentless changes of time could not be glossed over. The stone fireplace had been scrubbed clean and filled with a bank of electric logs, the old varnished wood bin removed to make room for a magazine table. A flat screen television stood in one corner, its satellite connection offering some link to the wider world. Mike picked up the remote and scrolled through the channels, but he soon turned the set off.

Syl remembered how it had been when she was younger, building fires here on rainy days, and reading, and working on whatever jigsaw puzzle had been started. She remembered the old jukebox, and the soda machine that vended bottles. She had never missed watching TV then.

At least the bearskin still hung on the wall, and a faded map of the lake drawn in 1973, and the deer antlers, and a taxidermized marten. The wall lamps were still made of birch logs, and there was still a random assortment of puzzles and left-behind books stacked on a narrow set of shelves.

Here is where Syl first read *To Kill a Mockingbird*, on a rainy day like this one, curled up on the wood-framed sofa beneath the windows. She'd finished it in one sitting.

Mike looked around at the room, picked up a fishing magazine, put it down again.

"Could we get out of here for a while? Go into town?"

Syl kept her eyes on the books, searching for something she knew was gone.

"The nearest real town is Northbrook. It's about half an hour. There's a Foodland that's open 24 hours, but not a whole lot else. Well, a beer store," she said.

She remembered when the lodge had been busy enough to supply the guests with beer, with cases stacked behind the garage to be delivered as requested. But the lodge was winding down, with no children in the family to continue it, no advertising to draw in new business, no improvements to the buildings and services. No more lunches served, no more daily housekeeping. All the sinks had been removed from the cabins because it was no longer acceptable to pump in untreated lake water for washing up, even though everyone who came here knew not to drink it.

Syl spotted a slender red book tucked in among the throwaway novels and reached up to pull it down. *Away Back in Clarendon and Miller* was the only local history book she had ever seen on the area. Her mother had once had a copy of it, a gift from Catherine MacHugh.

#

Catherine MacHugh had been born Catherine Mueller, the middle daughter from the first fertile wife of the lodge's founder. Catherine and her husband, Tom MacHugh, took over the lodge after Howard Mueller's death in 1972. Their children, Arnold and Grace, both unmarried and childless, took over the lodge in their own turn.

The lodge family history Syl learned had been Howard and Margie, then Catherine and Tom, then Arnold and Grace. Syl never knew Catherine's mother's name. Howard's first wife was like a ghost, not spoken of among the guests.

But his second was, and vividly. Margie MacDonald was a party girl from a comfortable Toronto family, bright and vivacious and athletic. Howard Mueller met her on a business trip, and convinced her to marry him and move to the wilds of Ontario's highlands.

Margie used to swim out to the point every morning from late spring until autumn. Margie liked the privacy of her morning swim, away from the clamor of the kitchen and the demands of the men. In the water, Margie was free of her earthly weight and too far out to answer if anyone called her. She was not afraid of the lake, or its weeds.

#

The rain ended during dinner, but Syl wanted to stay in the common room for a while. She paged through an old *Reader's Digest*, passing time as the daylight faded. Mike went back to the cabin to watch videos on his phone, bored in the silence. With him gone Syl realized the lodge was empty, even the kitchen cleaned and dark. But Syl wasn't ready to settle yet.

She made her way down to the big dock and sat in one of the wet, weathered Adirondack chairs at its end, the lights of the lodge at her back, aware of the black water that stretched away around her. The sky above was enormous, dark and deep and dusted with stars. Looking up, she reminded herself that she was seeing the Milky Way, that it was always there. She tilted her head back against the chair's back and waited for a shooting star.

A light wind ruffled the water and brushed like a spiderweb against her cheek. Watching the stars was not enough of a distraction. She felt isolated, laid bare under such a wide sky. She wished there were more people in camp this week. The quiet was enough to drown in. She was certain that something watched her, waiting for its chance.

Syl turned to look down the path of the moonlight on the water. A dark shape bobbed along on the white-lit ripples, drifting toward the dock. It looked like a small, round head held above the water. She broke out in an icy sweat, rose and walked as quickly and softly as she could back to land.

And then she ran, her gait flat-footed and strange to accommodate the uneven ground, her knees loose to absorb the impact. She was sure of the terrain, but the slippery grass beneath her feet slowed her down. She would not look behind her.

She couldn't help but think of a lodge story she had always heard told as a joke, of the night back in '62 that Charlie Kormutter ran his boat full-speed into the big dock while coming back from Bingo Bay. They always said he was drunk. They never said why he was in such a hurry.

It was years later, long after he'd given up night fishing, that he said he'd seen the baby.

#

The baby. There were oblique references to the baby in a few of the camp stories, but as the older guests died off the references were less often repeated. The stories still got told, worn down to jokes now with no hint of warnings.

Except for one, that Syl overheard accidently when she was seven or eight. The adults didn't know she was still awake, didn't realize how clearly their low voices carried in the quiet night as they sat on the cabin's porch, drinking whiskey and retelling themselves the camp's darker rumors.

They said that Margie was so used to her morning solitude she did not notice her small daughter follow her to the lake's edge and into the water. At least, they said, that's what must have happened. The baby was in her cot in the house when Margie left for her swim, and gone when Margie waded back onto shore.

One of the kitchen girls thought she had seen a white shape in the water while she set the dining room for breakfast, but she couldn't be sure. It might have been light striking off the water. The baby was never found, although Howard and the neighbors crossed and recrossed the lake for any sign of her, and combed the woods with their hunting dogs without any hope.

They said Maggie stopped swimming to the Point for a long time. They said she told Catherine she was afraid of finding the baby there in the weeds. Catherine was still a teenager then, and had filled in the blank mystery with wild imagination. Catherine had said she pictured the baby's face swollen with water, her eyes open and her fat young fingers wrapped around the weeds.

And everyone knew that was why Catherine would not swim at all.

#

Syl had only tried to swim to the Point once, when she was fifteen. No one warned her not to.

Syl grew up knowing that you did not go near the dump at dusk, and you did not go to the sandpit alone. But the weeds—she didn't learn that until she was in them.

She and a girl up from Ohio whose name was lost to memory had set out from the big dock with Syl's brother in a rowboat beside them. At first it seemed fun, an adventure, but when the girls reached the weed bed they both began screaming at the slimy fronds stroking their legs, and scrambled panicking into the boat to be rowed back to shore.

After that, Syl refused to swim outside the small bathing area, with its clean sand bottom and clear water. She claimed she was afraid of the big pike in the lake, and the snapping turtles, but that wasn't the truth. She was afraid of what she couldn't see.

#

She didn't like being out in a boat either, especially at dusk. The lake was inscrutable then, between reflection and darkness, and the boat such a small thing to float upon it. But sometimes her father insisted she and her brothers come out with him, for company.

As a child, Syl preferred to fish off the short dock across from the boathouse, casting into the shallow weed bed there for perch and sunnies, a step from the shore. Once, she had caught a pike, lithe and slimy and too small to keep. More often, she caught only weeds.

Her father always sought out the pike and the largemouth bass, the weedy spots and the monsters that lurked in them. He was not deterred by the fronds that tangled his lures and stripped off his bait, or his daughter's nervous complaints.

This was, after all, the Land O' Lakes, and he was here to fish. When nothing was biting on Kashwakamak, her father would leave camp to fish at Marble Lake, or Skootamatta, or Little Mink, but then he went with other fishermen and the kids stayed behind with their mother. Rarely, he would bring his children on the rough mile-long hike into Mannerheim, which he stubbornly called Monahan's.

Syl hated that hike. The path cut up and over a steep ridge to a swampy lake surrounded by rock walls. The mosquitoes were always thick, and if the water was high there was no shoreline. Syl remembered being trapped on a muddy patch at the edge of the lake, waiting until her father would declare defeat and bring them back to the lodge.

#

Like every cabin at Long Lake Lodge, cabin 9 faced the water. Syl latched the screen door as soon as it shut behind her and slid the wide porch windows closed, but the glass seemed an inadequate shield against what might be in the dark.

The moon had followed her, and made a fresh path to the short dock in front of her cabin.

She turned away before she could see a round shape floating there, if it had followed her too. The baby must be there in the mud beneath the tangled logs above the dam, Syl thought, drifted to a stopping place on the slow lake currents.

Mike snored from the darkness of the bedroom. Syl climbed quietly into the depths of the narrow second bed and pulled the red wool blanket over her head.

The bell rang again that night, long after the camp was quiet, swaying in the inconstant wind.

#

"Mike," Syl said over breakfast, "let's leave camp for a while today. I want to head over toward Plevna."

Mike sipped his coffee. "Why? What's there?"

"I want to go to the cemetery where Grace and Arnold's family is buried. It's not far."

Mike looked out over the lake. In the bright morning sun, it reflected the wide blue sky.

"Sounds fun," he said.

Syl followed his gaze toward the water.

There was only one other family here this week, and they had already finished eating and left the dining room. They didn't seem to stay in camp during the day. Syl missed the years when the dining room was full, and the conversations stretched across multiple tables.

Voices drifted out from the kitchen, punctuated by the clink of dishes. She heard Grace call out to one of the other women, teasing, and then a burst of laughter.

"I'll drive," Syl said.

#

St. Killian's Cemetery was a narrow swath along Road 509 marked by a faded sign, laid plain under the wide sky with no trees among the graves to offer shade. A waist-high chain-link fence set back about twenty feet from the road marked its boundary.

There was no parking lot, no paved path snaking through a crowd of grave markers, no benches for visitors. Here it was only a field and scattered stones. Syl parked in front of the gate, where the scrubby grass had been worn away.

"I'll wait here," Mike said, not looking at her.

Syl looked at her hands, still holding the wheel.

"I won't be long," Syl said after a moment, and climbed out of the car.

Syl had been here once, years ago, when Tom had died. It took her a minute to find his grave again. She remembered it being closer to the road than it was. Now, she saw, Catherine's name had been added beside her husband's.

Catherine had been dead for five years already. Syl didn't think that much time had passed.

Syl bent down to read the dates again. Tom had died twelve years ago. She could remember him so clearly, more clearly than she remembered Catherine.

Visitors had left pebbles on the headstones. Syl thought it was only a Jewish tradition, but it seemed important here as well. She found a chip of granite and placed it on the ledge made by the stone's base, careful to set it midway between the names. She offered no prayers.

When she stood again, she glanced back at the car. Mike's head was tilted down, either asleep or engrossed in his phone.

She cast about for Howard and Margie's grave. It wasn't far from Catherine's, in a cluster of headstones all engraved with *Mueller*.

There were no stones on this one.

Syl stared at the headstone, at the graven names, at the dates so far in the past she hadn't been born yet. She glanced at the surrounding markers, looking for a child's grave. There was nothing that fit the story, no buried child close-by that could have been Margie's.

She walked quickly up and down the long cemetery, looking for any small headstone that might be the one. Maybe, she thought, there was no body to bury.

Before she went back to the car, she scratched a rock out of the dirt and laid it on Howard and Margie's headstone. It looked strange, all by itself.

She wondered if anyone would visit and notice.

#

Syl went into the kitchen after breakfast was done, circling the lodge to use the back door. She hoped to catch Grace alone, but there was an old woman still with her, peeling potatoes for dinner.

"Sylvia, hello!" Grace said, coming toward her. "I'm so glad you made it up this year with your friend. How are you?"

"I'm good, Grace. It's been hard since Dad died, but I'm really glad to be up here."

Grace smiled. Syl shifted her weight.

"Look, Grace, I need to ask you something." Syl glanced around the familiar kitchen, hoping the woman inside couldn't hear.

"Sure," Grace said, a small frown creasing her forehead.

"I went to the cemetery yesterday. I found your grandparents' graves, but I didn't find any marker for the baby."

Grace looked at her, the frown deepening. "What baby?"

Syl realized that she didn't know Grace well at all after so many years, not well enough for this question. Syl reached out for Grace's hand so she wouldn't pull away. "The one who drowned. The one who followed Margie out into the lake and drowned."

"There was no baby," Grace said quickly. "There never was a baby."

Syl blinked.

"But... I saw something, in the water, off the big dock. What about Charlie Kormutter? What about the stories Margie told your mother? Please, Grace," Syl begged. She heard her own voice rising with frustration.

Grace tugged her hand loose. "Sylvia, stop it."

The woman peeling potatoes had stopped her task to watch them. Syl felt her cheeks flare red.

"That's an old yarn some of the men used to spin just to scare the kids. There never was a baby. Margie never had a baby. I didn't know anyone believed that."

Syl slumped and turned away.

"I'm sorry," she said. "I saw something in the water. I remembered the story."

Grace smiled at her, tight and cool. "Probably a beaver," she said. "No one has drowned here since the lodge has been here. No ghosts."

"I'm sorry," Syl said again, and fled.

#

When she got back to the cabin, she saw that the car was gone. Mike had left a note on the porch table—*Gone to find Northbrook, don't wait up.*

She crumpled up the paper and put it in the recycling can. It was barely noon.

Syl was too restless to stay in the cabin, or pass the day in the lodge. She went back out into the sunlight. The sky was so bright, and the wind so warm. The air smelled clean. It was a beautiful day. She closed her eyes and forced herself to bask in it, to prove that this was why she had come back. The camp was quiet around her, yet she did not feel alone. She felt as if something was just behind her, ready to reach out and touch her arm. She opened her eyes.

It was only the camp, and the trees, and the lake before her.

She wandered down to the lake, trailing along the line of logs protecting the grassy edge, past cabins set deep in shade. As she reached the far side of the camp, she climbed up to the overgrown road behind the MacHughs' house, thinking of ticks when the grass brushed her legs. Birch leaves rustled like paper in the high wind, turning to show their silver.

The trees were thin through here. She could see the yellow cabins scattered along the curve of the lake, and the soft green banks of moss growing on the shingled roofs.

If she followed the road to its end she would reach the swamp, a pocket in the lake shore where the currents never reached.

Sweat stung her eyes, and she wiped it away. She wished Mike were here with her. She wished Mike were interested in being here with her.

She kept going, the sense of another presence growing as she got closer to the end of the road. The grass gave way to a stand of horsetail reeds and listing cedars and birch. She used to catch bullfrogs here, years ago. She had expected to hear their croaks and heavy splashes. But the small cove was only full of rotten logs and cattails, and utterly quiet except for the wind. She looked around slowly.

From the corner of her eye, she saw something move. She turned, trying to track it. Wind ruffled the curling shreds of bark that clung to a broken birch stump. Her stomach knotted, knowing what was here.

Syl stumbled back as the bark of the splintered birch peeled away with a sudden gust, unfurling as a tattered dress around the wasted form of a small child. A child whose mouth was wide, and red, and empty. The child raised its arms to her, begging to be lifted. It stepped toward her.

"No!" Syl cried, her voice echoing off the trees. She shut her eyes and struck out at the small figure, scraping her hands on rough bark. She felt it break and crumble beneath her flailing hands. She heard herself screaming, her voice jagged in terror.

She thrashed at the air until she lost her balance and fell to the muddy ground, then wrapped her arms around her head and cried, waiting to feel a cold small hand on her cheek. She heard startled voices, far off but coming closer. She heard the hard thud of running feet.

She opened her eyes.

There in the mud and tangled roots before her, tiny teeth like chips of ivory grinned up in a scattered smile.

Fallen

SARAH'S SISTER WAS watching the baby for her again. Sarah had told her that she had to work. It was another one of her little lies. Her life was littered with them.

Sarah was supposed to work, but she had called out sick again. It was late summer, and the flower shop was deadly slow. She hated the boredom, so it wasn't much of a stretch to say she had a headache again. What was one more little lie?

Besides, she had something else she wanted to do, up on the mountain.

Sarah had grown up in the shadow of Garrett Mountain, like everyone else she knew in Richfield. The mountain's presence was as much of a given as air, no matter what part of town a kid came from. Her father told stories of when he was a boy, going camping with his cousins up in the reservation, eating wild blueberries and fishing in Barbour's Pond. When she was young her father took her and her siblings up into the wilder parts, and showed them where the blueberry bushes grew, and how sassafras twigs tasted like root beer.

She thought about that as she pulled onto the side street that jutted off the main road up the mountain, and rolled past the last, lonely house to the blunt dead end where trees overhung the pavement and weeds had swallowed the curbs. There were no blueberry bushes here, and the sassafras were swallowed by maples. A chain hung across the overgrown entrance between two peeling yellow posts, but a narrow foot path snaked around it and followed the old roadcut back to the abandoned quarry pit.

When her father was a boy, the quarry had been active, and off-limits. At least, that is what he had told her. She had the feeling it wasn't the truth.

She got out and looked around to make sure no one was watching her. She couldn't see any movement on the street. A car passed by on the main road, and then quiet resumed. The air hung hot and silent. She locked her car and walked quickly past the posts. As she made her way along the path, the noises of the city faded away behind her. She heard birds chirp and flit in the trees above her, and the scuttle of small animals in the high grass bordering the trail.

And then the cover of vegetation fell away and she was looking up at the high rock walls that bounded the lonely place.

The saplings at the base of the cliff rattled in a breeze she couldn't feel, their dusty leaves rustling with a steady, faint whisper. She followed the thin trail along the shoulder of the cliff until it petered out among the weeds.

The quarry was bigger than she remembered, and more isolated. Sarah felt like the only person in the world.

She stood for a long while on the edge of the pit floor, listening to the wind move through the grass and the slender trees that had sprung up in clusters across the expanse. Without the shade of the trail, the late morning sun beat down on her. She turned her face up to bask in it, closing her eyes, seeing the sun glow through her eyelids. She thought she could feel her skin turning brown beneath the heavy light.

She remembered the breathless, adolescent rumors of devil worship on the mountain and of biker gangs hanging out at the quarry, but under the bright August sun the stories seemed as far away as junior high. Dave had brought her here once, a couple years ago, because the rumors and stories were as close as she had ever been to the quarry when she was a teen. They climbed up at the low part of the wall, and walked along the rim and through the cut in the fence to the overgrown bluff behind the university parking lot. It had been exciting to have Dave show her around, even if she was really too old for it. She hadn't thought about Ronny then.

But Dave wasn't here now. And Ronny was all she could think of.

#

The winter that Sarah was in eighth grade, Ronny Cornelius had died up here.

A few weeks ago, Sarah had been leafing through her ninth-grade yearbook, looking over the class pictures of friends she no longer spoke to, wondering what had gone wrong with her life. One of the last pages of the maroon volume was dedicated to Ronny. She had been surprised. She hadn't thought about that winter in so long. She hadn't thought about him.

It had been ten years already. So much time gone by, with little to show for it.

Sarah had never expected to live this long. She thought she would be gone by eighteen, because she couldn't envision what would happen to her after her mother died. But she had persisted, somehow. Now she was divorced, with a toddler, and living back home with her dad and younger sisters. This is not the life she thought she would have, back when she was fifteen.

But it was more than Ronny ever got.

#

When Ronny disappeared, no one at school knew it right away. For those first couple of days, he was just absent.

All the kids knew that sometimes somebody would run away up onto Garrett Mountain, hiding out up by the folly above the castle until they felt like going home, or staying down on the horse trails. The reserve wasn't big enough to get lost in, but it was big enough to play at it. Sometimes kids just stayed out too late hanging out in the quarry, smoking and drinking and pretending at being badasses.

But kids didn't usually stay out on the mountain too late just for fun in January, when it was still cold and snowy and grey. Not unless something was really wrong.

By the end of the week, Ronny's parents had gone to the newspapers, and then everyone knew he was missing.

#

Sarah hadn't really known Ronny, except as someone she passed in the halls sometimes. They lived across town from each other. They went to different elementary schools. She didn't have any classes with him when they got to junior high. She had other concerns. But the morbid allure of someone her age disappearing drew her in like a trap. Every day, she read the papers to cull any new scrap of information that she could add to the general gossip at school. There was very little to be had. The gossip spun on without it, creating competing rumors that he had run off to New York, that he was a Satanist, that he had been kidnapped for ransom.

The newspapers repeated themselves almost daily for the first couple of weeks Ronny was missing, prodded by his distraught family. But with nothing new, the reports tapered off to the occasional mention, the suggestion of a new search to be done, the offer of a psychic to assist, the pleas of Ronny's mother for help, any help at all. It became embarrassing to read after a while.

Then as winter loosened its grip and the world started to thaw, Ronny's body fell from the crevice that held it, and the great mystery was gone.

At least for Sarah.

#

She didn't know how long ago the quarry had been closed down. Maybe Ronny's death had been the tipping point for the quarry operator, a reason to walk away.

There hadn't been any trucks or mining equipment in here in a long time, the entry road become just a wide grassy swath as nature filled in the damage. The only remaining evidence of the former business was a decrepit trailer that had been left behind in the pit, a solitary landmark among the patchy weeds.

She approached the trailer slowly, making her way to it through the maze of garbage and rotted-out oil drums scattered across the area. Rust had eaten holes in the trailer's sides and top. Spray-painted swastikas and other aggressive graffiti splashed across the remaining sheet metal. One door stood wide open, while the other hung by its top hinge. She could see litter and old blankets inside the trailer's shell, and kept her distance.

As Sarah circled the trailer, she stepped around a ring of stones that held the remains of a recent fire. Around it lay a wide scattering of empty beer bottles and cans of various ages. Broken glass, green and brown, sparkled among the weeds. Plenty of people still came up here, she realized. She reassured herself that they came at night, but she looked around with new awareness, making sure she was still alone. There were no human sounds here, only the tapping of branches moved by wind. She wondered if Ronny had come here too, to see the remains of parties he hadn't attended, before he climbed, and fell.

With a thrill of nervousness, Sarah moved away from the wreckage of the trailer and scanned the high rock walls, wondering at how close the city still was to this desolate place. Shading her eyes against the sun, she could see antennas and slivers of rooftop above the pit's lip. The city was all around, but this place was lonely. It would always be lonely. That is what drew everyone who came.

She moved her gaze lower, at the thin ledges and deep vertical cracks in the cliff, and wondered which crevice had been Ronny's grave.

As she stood below the towering rocks, she pulled a folded paper from her pocket and reread the blurry photocopy of an old newspaper article she had dug up in the library.

The body of a fifteen-year-old boy who has been missing since January was found yesterday in a local quarry, at the base of a seventy-five-foot cliff, only yards from where he was last seen alive. A truck driver for the quarry found the body. Police said the boy's body apparently fell after it became dislodged from a crevice in the basalt cliffs that form the western face of Garrett Mountain. Authorities labeled the death an accident. Police said they and quarry employees had checked the area where the body was found numerous times in the weeks following the boy's disappearance on January 30.

She had read it so often over the past few days, she could nearly recite it. She wondered if they had recovered all of his bones.

#

The stones that had fallen at the base of the cliff wall made it easier to begin her climb. She wiped her hands dry on her jeans and looked for the most promising place to start. The hot sun baked her hair and her black t-shirt.

She could have climbed up near the entrance, where the quarry walls sloped down to only eight or ten feet high, and displaced boulders made rough steps. But to do that would be to avoid the risks, and weaken the experience. She wanted the danger while she mulled over Ronny's end.

She dug her sneakered toe into the pitted rock face and reached for the first handhold her gripping fingers could find. She smelled baby powder and acrid sweat as she raised her arms to pull herself up.

At times she moved sideways across the uneven rock until she could find a path to move up again. Her clothes became smeared with red dust as she pressed into the cliff. Her fingers grew sore from the friction.

She climbed like a slow spider up the rock wall until she reached a narrow ledge where she could rest and look over the expanse of the pit. This had been a small quarry, and set where it was on the mountain the pit had never filled with water. Instead it was littered with fallen chunks of rock and clumps of grass, like an empty lot. It looked even more bleak from a height.

Sarah smacked her lips together to get some saliva flowing. She hadn't thought to bring anything to drink. But she was nearly to the top. She resumed climbing, and was relieved when she finally heaved herself over the lip and stood on solid ground again.

Up here, she couldn't even hear the cars on Valley Road.

Sarah walked along the curved rim of the pit, peering down to see if she could tell from above which spot had hidden Ronny's body for almost two months. Behind her, a chain-link fence obscured with brush and tall trees marked the limits of the quarry property, a reminder of how close the world still was. She could see the backyard of an enormous new home on the other side of the wire links, green and well-kept, with a patio and a pool and a high, white wrought-iron fence of its own to keep the house apart from the quarry's mess. The house had wonderful views of the mountain, and the city below it.

Sarah looked back down at the dusty weeds in the pit.

She wondered what it would feel like to fall into it.

#

Sarah finished her exploration along the cliff top with nothing to show for it. Sweating and tired, she sat down away from the edge and reread the news clipping again, looking for clues that it did not contain. After reading it again she let the paper drop into her lap and squinted up at the sun. She had gotten here around ten, she thought. It had to be close to noon. She was thirsty, and the skin on her arms and neck felt tight. A bead of sweat rolled off the tip of her nose and splashed onto the paper.

She cursed beneath her breath, at herself, at the article, wiping the sweat away. She wasn't going to find the spot where Ronny died. She stuffed the article back into her pocket, suddenly uncomfortable with what she was doing here. She had turned into a creep, a ghoul, this whole adventure built on the memory of a boy she had never been friends with. If she had been, if she had known him at all, she wouldn't be here.

She wished she and Dave were still together, that she hadn't been stupid, and lied, and goaded him to break up with her. She had just wanted to feel alive. She hadn't cared that it would hurt.

She got up, ashamed with how she had gotten to this point, and wandered back and forth until her head felt clear. Then she lowered herself over the cliff's edge and started the long climb down.

It was harder than the climb up had been. She peered down between her body and the rock wall she clung to, anxious for the ground. Her hands grew muddy with dust and sweat. Her biceps burned from holding her weight as she felt blindly with her foot for the next step down.

After what seemed like far longer than it should take, she glanced down to see that she had nearly reached the bottom again. She paused and braced herself to wipe sweat from her bleared eyes, and shifted her weight as she reached down for the next handhold.

As she moved, her foot slipped from the tiny bump of rock she balanced on, and for a sickening few seconds she hung by her fingers before she lost her grip and crashed down the final dozen feet onto the thick, dry weeds.

She lay stunned, staring into the bright sky for what seemed like a day before she could struggle up onto her feet. The pain across her back was sharp and bruising, and her ribs ached as she drew in shallow breaths. She slumped against the rock wall for balance, and waited for her head to stop spinning before trying to stand straight. Her body protested. She felt the back of her head for damage, but her fingers came away without blood. Broken twigs stuck in her hair and scratched at her neck like sharp fingers. She reached up to pull them out, ripping out snarled strands of her hair with them. She looked at the twigs in her hand. They were as pale and bleached as old bones. She threw them away. She didn't want to be here anymore.

Dry red stones clattered suddenly down on her, striking her shoulders and head. She jumped away from the cliff, clumsy and lightheaded. After the stones, a scarecrow-shaped collection of sticks rattled down.

The twigs and branches scraped along the rock wall as they fell, slowing as they tangled in the weeds growing from seams in the rock. The bundle of broken branches came apart, its form dispersed, cracked wooden ribs left behind, caught in long grasses, splintered wooden arms and legs disarticulated as they reached the ground in a heap of brush.

She looked up, searching for whoever had thrown the debris at her. The cliff edge was empty.

Without thinking, Sarah stumbled away from the rock face, turned until she found her bearings, and headed across the open pit floor toward the gap of the old roadcut. The sun was a burden, pressing down on her.

Saplings knocked together by a hot wind filled the quarry with a dry clicking and a rustle like low voices. The sound echoed and faded only to swell again on a fresh gust. The clicking followed her, close at her back. She fought the need to run, in pain and afraid of tripping and falling with the sound of tapping sticks filling her ears.

As she limped across the wide, exposed field, the wind swept down and across it, buffeting her, plucking at her hair and clothes with invisible fingers, flinging dust and bits of broken grass stems at her retreating form. The doors of the trailer swung in the wind, closing with a hollow boom. She tried to turn her head, to look behind her, but the blowing grit made her squint against it, and she could not be sure if she saw a scarecrow figure behind her or if she imagined it.

She realized that no one knew she was here. She walked faster, pushing her aching body toward the path out of this grave.

She had made a mistake. She needed to get home, to get back to her baby and her boring job, to the unmanageable life she still had. The beginning of the trail eluded her, and she fought through the high weeds that filled the roadcut. The way out seemed far harder than the way in.

She broke into a run when she saw the yellow posts, and lurched out onto the road. She did not look back. As she reached her car, she dug in her pocket for her keys. The folded paper popped out with them. She picked it up from the dirty pavement and tore it into bits that she threw back down. The white flecks tumbled along the street on the warm wind, catching in the weeds.

The branches of the overhanging trees clattered in the same wind. She got in the car, locked the doors, and pulled away.

He was someone else's ghost. She didn't belong here with him.

Here Is Where Your Proud Waves Halt

ASTER WENT TO the seaside at the end of autumn, to bear her child in peace. No one bothered much with the coast since things had changed. She had not told her family she was going; it was better they were behind her, with their sharp questions, their wants and needs. Their superstitions. Their claims on her. I refute you, she thought. All of you. At the edge of the land she could be alone except for the constant song of the sea, to ready herself as best she could.

She stopped where the pavement disappeared, smothered by drifting sand. Her car still had nearly a quarter tank of gasoline, but she was done driving. The roads were broken and lonely. She could not escape the conviction that some terrible thing rode with her. She hoped it was only the dread of the new.

The town where she stopped was called Ocean Gate, and it was nearly empty. The houses along the main street stood shuttered against the season, and all but one greasy-windowed convenience store was closed. Before, even this late in the year there would have been more people about. But before was behind her, with her family. Now Aster stood on the sandy pavement, letting the wind push at her back, and looked around as the dusk gathered down. Here and there she could see a dim light come on, a sparse handful among bungalows crowded in like teeth. It was what she expected.

She pulled up to one of the tiny holiday cottages that huddled in accelerating decline on the near side of the dunes. The cottage had once been a seafoam green before years of benign neglect had faded the color to a shadow. It was near the entrance to the long amusement pier that stretched out in rotting grandeur over the beach and into the waves, near what remained of Ocean Gate's town center. She broke the lock and hauled her bags in from the car, and took stock of the shoddy, vacation-home furnishings. From the other lights in town, she knew there was still power. The electric heat smelled of burning dust when she turned it on.

#

Her son was born alive at midwinter after two days of labor. He only lasted for a few hours. He did not suckle. She was not surprised. She did not name him.

When his breathing stopped, she gathered up the bloody bedclothes and bundled his small body in them, disguising him under layers of cloth, a cocoon for his transformation from being to object. Then she lay down with him on the bare, sagging mattress and finally slept. Her dreams could not cut through her exhaustion, but they informed her.

When she awoke in the afternoon, she walked stiffly to the beach and gave him to the waters.

As the tide drew the small, wrapped body down and away, the water scraped clean a glistening oval that had been buried in the grey sand. Her grief still too distant to touch, Aster pulled it up and wiped it off on her wet skirts.

It was a mirror, as big as her palm and set in a black frame of tarnished silver. She could see something in the glass, a reflection that was not hers. She held it closer to her eyes, then startled and let it fall from her cold fingers. The image of her infant son's face laughing up at her was erased by a flash of white sunlight caught in the glass.

Addicted, Aster wanted that image back. She scrambled after the mirror, afraid the sea would sweep it away as well. As she grabbed it, a sharp edge of the frame sliced across her fingers. Bright blood drew a line that dripped onto the wet sand. The glass reflected only her face and the empty sky behind her. She shuddered, suddenly burdened with a sense of being noticed, being known.

She looked at the sea but the water was empty. Her son was gone. She wrapped her fingers carefully around the mirror and held it against her heart as she walked back up the beach.

She went back to her bungalow, locked all the doors, drew all the shades. When darkness fell, she tried to sleep again, but her son's living face laughed at her when she closed her eyes. Aster felt suddenly sure that he knew where she was. It was no comfort.

#

Days passed in slow, solitary motion, became a week, became two. Aster's body still ached from the fruitless birth. She still bled. She slept in fragments. At night the ocean called her, its dull growl the only sound in the quiet dark.

She did not need a lamp with the moon falling bright through her carelessly covered windows. She pulled on loose sweatclothes and left the shelter of the tiny cottage for the wide, cold beach. The wind was sharp. Broken black threads of seaweed sketched the line of the tide. All the shells she saw were shards. The mirror was a weight in her pocket.

As she waded into the tide, the wind bit her where her clothes were soaked. She knew she needed to be in the sea. She pulled out the mirror and clutched it in one stiff hand, turning it to catch what it would. All the glass reflected was scattered moonlight. Her legs grew numb, but she felt the warm, wormy trickle of blood between her cold thighs.

I will grow my hair out into hag's weeds, she thought madly. I will starve myself down to a whip, beyond the matters of meat and bone, beyond the limits of flesh. I will bring you back. Her lips moved over the words. Her eyes burned with tears.

Still, the mirror was empty. Aster waited a few more minutes for some sign or direction. None came. She slogged out of the sea and back across the sand to her house.

#

In the late spring, like blossoms, a few families came down from the inland towns to show their children what had been, drawn by nostalgia and old habit. They came with loaded cars, with coolers and sand toys, folding chairs and swimsuits. It was too chill and grey for swimming, but that did not prevent the wide-eyed children from running up and down the long empty beach until the misty sun began to slip away. When it did the sunsets were brilliant, slashes of gold and coral and violet across the deepening sky.

To Aster's amazement, a handful of stalls opened on the pier as soon as the vacationers appeared, selling what plastic junk they had left from other, brighter years. A perpetual smell of sweet grease hung over the single food stall.

Aster, nostalgic herself, joined in by setting up her own shop in what had been a fortune teller's booth. She found old nets and draped them on the walls, filling them with whatever the sea threw up to her. She wrapped herself in layers of loose clothes and any bright jewelry she could find. She rimmed her cloudy blue eyes with smeared dark liner, teased her silver-shot black hair into a cloud, turned her dark skin to ash under powder. She felt safer in her costume, less watched.

Enough people still yearned for magic that she stayed the whole brief season. She would lean in to her visitors, and hold up the mirror as if she were taking a selfie with them, whispering nonsense the entire time. Sometimes she saw things that shouldn't be there. More often she invented them, spun stories like candy floss. Her visitors saw what she told them was there. Some hoped for more.

#

"Sylvia. Ah. And what are we asking for now?"

"I want to know—"

"No. Don't say it."

Sylvia had been to see Aster several times over several weeks, always with vague, empty questions that anyone could nudge into an answer. She seemed attached to the exotic lie Aster offered. It was clear she was lonely. She was very young. Aster remembered being so young, so lonely.

Sometimes Sylvia offered her old dirty cash, sometimes packaged foods. Once, Sylvia pressed a brooch made of dried flowers and lucite into Aster's hand.

"Look," she had said. "It's your name in there. The aster."

And, indeed, the faded blue flower was her name.

Now Aster leaned close, her cheek against Sylvia's. She held the mirror up before them, cupping it safely in her hand, turning it until she looked into her own eyes.

Aster drew a sharp breath.

"What is it? What do you see?" Sylvia cried out excitedly.

Aster hushed her, looking again into the clouded glass. He looked back at her. He had her eyes.

"He is already here," she said.

Aster reached out to touch Sylvia's belly but stopped herself, letting her hand hover.

"Are you sure?" Sylvia asked. "We've been trying so long, and when everything changed I thought we should stop but Tom said we have to go on..."

Aster turned the mirror away, afraid to look again. She shoved the glass into her pocket, silent, thinking. Sylvia began to make small noises, upset.

"Will you be back next year?" Aster said to calm her. "Bring him to me then. I'll prepare something for him. To keep him safe in the world."

"I will," Sylvia said, rising reluctantly from the cushions, her eyes soft. "I promise."

She hesitated until Aster waved her dismissal. Then she pressed folded bills into Aster's hand, more symbolic than valuable, and ran away up the pier.

Aster tucked the money away. She pulled the mirror out and held it up again. Her own face looked back, but from a great and foggy distance. She watched as her mirror image turned away from her, to the sea that roiled behind her. She watched what her mirror-self did then, the gestures, the payment made. She remembered the patterns.

#

When the summer was gone and the chill of autumn rolled in, Aster stood on the rocks under the empty pier and slit open her palm.

As the blood ran, she swung her arm up to draw remembered lines in the air, spraying her own red blood into the sea. The drops fell, dissolved, disappeared into the great swallowing mouth of the ocean.

That night as the tide turned, she felt it swell within her, felt it rumble and turn. Alone in the dark in the tiny cottage, with only a stretch of sand between her and the vast black sea, Aster grew frightened. She did not know what exactly she had done.

#

The next year Sylvia came, but it was nearly the end of summer when she did. She was alone, and she walked into Aster's sea-damp stall without greeting her. She had done as Aster asked.

Without a word, Sylvia took a seat on a faded cushion and unwrapped her child. The thing was as dark and twisted as driftwood, and waved its thin arms helplessly as the blankets came away. It had no eyes. Its mouth was a pink hole in a wet leather face. It whined like a pup.

"This?" Aster said before she could catch herself.

Sylvia held the damaged thing out to Aster. "Here," she said. "You wanted me to bring him."

Aster kept her hands down, knotted her fingers in her lap to make them useless.

"His name is Ty," Sylvia said. "You said you would have something for him."

Aster stared, nodded.

"Why now?" Aster said.

Sylvia started to cry but choked it back. Ty made his own sounds.

"It wasn't safe anymore." She pulled the wrappings back over her dreadful child. "I should have come back sooner. I think being around them did this to him."

"Them?"

"The things. The things," Sylvia said. Aster did not press. She could not trust Sylvia's needs now.

"What did you make for him?" Sylvia said after a moment. "You said you'd make something to keep him safe."

"I remember," Aster said. She stood and went to a cabinet on the back wall. She opened the door carefully on its broken hinges, sorted through the bits she had collected over the past year. Her fingers closed around a bottle of multi-colored sand with a cork stopper, the kind of dross children made at booths on the boardwalk. Aster had added seawater to it, and a drop of blood, and when it dried it had made a crust of bright sand on the glass.

Aster held it out to Sylvia. "This," she said.

Sylvia took it, glanced at it, and put it in a pocket. She rewrapped her baby and walked carefully out of the booth. Aster could not help notice the black lines of blight that crawled up Sylvia's wrist.

#

Sylvia came for Aster again in the depths of the following winter, when the sand was frosted in snow and the sea was as grey as slate. She knocked at the bungalow door, and Aster let her in. She had expected this, if not so soon.

Sylvia's nose and upper lip were eaten away by blight, and the disease had begun to work on the lower rims of her eyes. It had moved quickly. She clutched a swaddled Ty to her, or what was left of him. Aster held her breath against the smell of spoiled meat.

She drew Sylvia into the living room and made her sit in a threadbare armchair. Sylvia grabbed at Aster's hand, not letting her move away, and then her dam burst and she cried like a child. Aster stood there until Sylvia stopped sobbing, then pulled her hand free.

"Give me that," Aster said, and reached for the damp mass of blankets Sylvia held against herself. For a moment Sylvia looked at her through glossed eyes, not understanding. Then she released Ty's body to Aster's keeping.

"We'll bury him in the morning," Aster said. The taste of death wrapped around her tongue and seeped down her throat. "He'll be all right on the porch until then."

And without waiting for a reaction from Sylvia, she took the small body out the back door of the bungalow and left it on the cracked slab patio. She tucked the blankets closely around it. She did not want to see.

When she went back in, Sylvia hadn't moved from the chair. Her coat was stained like a butcher's smock, and the rotten smell still hung in the air. Aster opened the front and side windows to let the cold wind clean the air.

"How did you get here?" Aster said, breathing deeply, shivering in her nightclothes.

"Drove. Then walked. I have nowhere to go," Sylvia said. "There's no one left who wants me."

Aster gave up and closed the windows again.

"How long have you had the blight?"

Sylvia looked away. "Before I was pregnant. That made it worse, I think."

#

After the morning's silent ceremony, Sylvia went back to the bungalow. Aster stayed behind to pray, she said, for Ty's safe passage. Once Sylvia was gone, Aster unearthed the sad shrunken body and gave it to the sea.

When Ty had sunk beneath the surface, Aster drew her sigils in the sand, calling. The waves came up but would not wash over them, swept in at an angle that left her marks behind. She drew the lines again, further down the sand, but still the sea refused to take them. When she sliced her finger deeply on the mirror's frame and retraced the lines in red, the sea came up, hungry, and wiped the sand clean.

She held the mirror steady to see what it reflected, careful not to smear it with blood. He was there, older. His dark hair was a mess, but his eyes burned clean.

Aster smiled to herself, and put the mirror away.

#

The winter wore on, longer than it had ever been. Aster found she didn't mind having Sylvia there. She was like a ghost in the tiny house, tragic and nearly invisible.

"What's left out there?" Aster asked her.

Sylvia cast her eyes down, shy or embarrassed. "Not much more than here," she said. "Everyone just sort of...went wandering off. The world is getting empty."

Aster went over to her then, put her arms around Sylvia's crumbling, bony shoulders. "We're still here," she said. "That's got to count for something."

Sylvia smiled wanly and shrugged.

"I have an idea," Aster said. "If the car starts, we can take a ride."

"To where?"

"Wherever."

Aster dug through the kitchen drawers until she found the keys. She bundled herself and Sylvia in sweatshirts and sweaters and coats, and tucked an old crocheted afghan around Sylvia once she was settled in the passenger seat.

"Ready?" Aster said. She felt a flutter of excitement at the thought of driving away. She turned the key. Silence. Not even the click of the starter. She tried again, turning the key harder, afraid it might snap. Her eyes blurred with tears, sudden and unwanted.

Sylvia sat quietly, breathing steam into the cold space of the car, until Aster finished crying and brought her back into the house.

#

The next day, while Sylvia still slept, Aster walked to the rotten end of the pier, where the pilings had broken and spilled part of the boardwalk down into the water. The remaining boards were spongy underfoot. She braced herself, as if her stance could save her if they collapsed.

She slit her palm open across the old scar and threw her blood into the sea, the salt of her veins enriching the salt in the water. A storm swirled up from nothing, the wind a solid force, sharp pellets of ice salting the pier and her hair. The wind caught in her hair, pulling it loose of its clips and spinning it into a twisted crown, catching on her cheap earrings and silver chains. In its howling the storm told her things, dredging them from the muddy deeps, sucking them away from farther shores.

But for all the frenzy of the storm, the sea itself lay calm and smooth before her, its swells as quiet as sleeping breath. Aster wiped ice from her eyes. Through the clear glass of the waters, she could see the sunless white face of a young boy, floating up toward the surface like a balloon. The boy's eyes opened beneath a film of water, blue as her own. His mouth opened, a grey oval, and inside, the reflection of her face.

She shrieked and covered her eyes, and the wind dropped away, the waves resumed their pulse. Aster climbed quickly back up the slick boards, away from what she had seen.

#

Sylvia died one dark morning, her face a filigree of black scabs and ash. Aster buried her in the wet sand under the pier. She would be safe there. Aster knew that no one would come to the pier anymore. There had been no lights in Ocean Gate since summer ended. That part of the world was over.

Sand from the grave clung to Aster's hands. She scrubbed it into the black threads of blight that knit their pattern on her own skin.

#

At last the weather turned, cold grey winter sliding into chill grey spring. Aster had given up on marking time. The mirror had shown her things she couldn't read, her son's face, her own, echoes of each other. She missed her nameless boy. She missed Sylvia. She went back to the sea.

The pier had suffered from the winter's storms. The farthest end where she had once stood had tumbled into the surf, the wood smashed into jagged fretwork. Aster went as far as she could. She breathed deeply. The air was still cold enough to hurt.

She sliced deep into her hand, ready to draw her bloody patterns in the air. But there was no blood. She was dry as salt. The blight had drained her.

The sea needed blood. It fed him. The sea would not return him without it. Her heart fluttered in her chest, the thought of such loss overwhelming.

She stumbled farther down the broken staircase of planking, splinters digging into her black, weathered hands. She had to reach the water. From the slumping end of the pier she threw the mirror into the sea, as far as she could, as deep as she could reach. The water closed over it, hiding it, and became as still as the glass it had swallowed. She waited.

Behind her, footsteps creaked and rang hollow on the crumbling boards as what made them climbed down. Aster stood still, impatient, her eyes on the sea. Sharp breath and the heat of another body fell on her naked neck. The water threw back a reflection of what stood with her. Cloudy blue eyes. Tangled black hair. He had grown up. She had read it right.

"Mother," he said. When he embraced her, it burned like acid, like an electric shock. His touch charred her skin and blackened the bones beneath. Her eyes stung without tears to shed. She had no more blood in her to quench the fire.

Signals

ESTELLA LAY AWAKE, searching her dark room with wide open eyes for the source of the sound. She could see the night sky where the window shade had crept up, a slice of deep violet showing bright against the black of the room. But the sky was quiet, and the streets below as well. She could think of nothing else in the close darkness that would make any noise. But she could hear a barely audible note, almost a chime, that she could not place.

She had heard the sound in the background of the television's blare, a flickering ring that she thought was a bad signal. She turned the set off and the sound persisted. Then she thought it might be a lightbulb starting to burn out, and dismissed it as an annoyance.

But now the lights were out, the apartment was silent, and the sound still intruded, intermittent, almost musical and low as a whisper. Each time Estella thought she had figured it out, it stopped, only to resume after a few minutes.

She got up and stood in the middle of her small room. She listened, breath held, waiting for the sound to repeat. She heard the distant creak of the house's timbers settling in the cool night, heard the *tick* and *ping* of the radiators.

And there, so faint she could not tell if it was the thrum of her own blood inside her ears, a ringing like struck crystal that sang out and faded and sang out again.

She gasped, then caught her breath in again, afraid of drowning the sound out. But it escaped her.

Estella went to the window and pulled the shade all the way up. There was too much light pollution to see any stars, but she knew they were there. She flicked her fingernail against the windowpane and listened to the dull *plink* on the glass. It was not the sound she wanted.

She crawled back into her bed, pulling the blankets up around her ears. The crinkle and scratch of her hair against the pillowcase kept her awake for a long while.

#

Waking was an effort. Estella wished she could call out sick, but it was easier to just push through the exhaustion.

She tuned in a dance music station for the commute, but she couldn't drown out the other music that floated just beneath it, sharp and full of dissonant quirks. She shut off the radio and listened to the traffic.

The office, when she dragged in, was a hive of distractions, with voices rising and falling, the crisp shuffle of papers across cubicle-farmed desks, the *click* and *tap* of data input over and over again. She sat down quickly and logged in, trying to erase the unnamed song in her head. Under her fingers a clear cadence took shape. She struck the keys harder, typing nonsense across the fields. There was a lullaby comfort in the repetitious sound.

A phone rang, jarring across her rhythm. She blinked, and hit cancel on the mess she had typed in.

Claudia sat at the desk across from her, and came in a few minutes late, as always. She turned on her desktop and opened her music stream. A dated pop song drifted up from the computer's speakers, the sharp synthesizers piercing the otherwise white noise of the office. As the song built up to its jangling chorus, the strange high sound once again wormed its way into Estella's attention. It flowed along with the music, amplified by it but not in tune with it, distant, like a far-off bell.

Estella felt it tugging at her, the parasite sound a lure for something larger.

"Claudia, could you turn that off?" she said, too loudly. "I've got a headache today."

"Yeah, sure," Claudia answered with her normal cheer. "Why'd you even come in?"

Estella smiled, knowing how haggard she looked. "Exactly," she said.

#

Tommy had been the one who followed Alex Jones and Coast To Coast AM and anything he could dredge up about Area 51, the one who bought all the lizard men and alien conspiracy crap. His interest had grown from a quirk to a hobby to an obsession, and was a large part of why Estella had finally kicked him out.

Tommy had also talked about the music of the spheres, as if it were something he could tune in if he just kept still enough. It was twisted into his theories about alien overlords and human-alien breeding programs and cover-ups, to the point where Estella let it all wash over her without paying attention to his ramblings.

But after last night, she couldn't stop thinking about some of the theories he had gone on about, how certain resonances could change things, alter perceptions, twist the inner workings of a human mind.

Tommy had gone too far out, she reminded herself. Tommy was nuts.

The work day eventually ended, and Estella escaped the limits of the office. The sky was already purple at five o'clock, and the wind carried a bite in it that hinted at snow. She sat in her car for a few minutes with the engine running, waiting for the heat to come. She watched other people get into their own cars and drive off to join the crush of rush hour traffic. She didn't realize she was drowsing until a high, trembling note started her out of her trance.

She looked around the half-empty garage for the source of it, but it seemed to come from somewhere close to her. Inside the car. Inside her head. The note rose and fell like an intonation before it faded.

She shivered. She might have made sense of it, if it had gone on.

She turned on news radio and cranked up the heat, filling the car with chatter and moving air and pushing away the idea that she had inherited some of Tommy's crazy.

She didn't want to be nuts too.

#

At home and safe inside her own walls, Estella searched out some of the sites Tommy had followed. None of them were on the first page of the searches, but she dug them out. What she uncovered was a cross-section of rabid dogma decked out in 1990s graphics, with yellow and red font splashed across black backgrounds and obviously shopped photos screaming for attention. Other sites were much more professional looking, but the prose was still riddled with paranoia.

She read them all, websites, blogs, subreddit threads. She followed links within pages. The message boards were the worst. The conviction disturbed her more than the content. She felt herself sinking slowly into the fearful mindset that generated such bleak conspiracies. But following their logic required a leap of faith she would not make.

It was nearly four in the morning before she closed her laptop. She didn't feel healthy after what she had read. Thin, spitting rain hit the window in a rapid *tick-tick-tick*. She tried not to find any pattern in it.

#

Estella called out of work the next day, claiming a migraine.

The house felt different during the day, like a bubble of empty space with her apartment floating on top. She slept on and off through the morning, restless, knowing what she was going to do, and knowing it was a mistake to do it.

She had deleted Tommy's number after they broke up. She scrolled through her contacts, trying to figure out which shared friend would be the least inquisitive. Finally, she called Maria.

"I don't think he has a phone anymore. I think it's turned off. I haven't tried to call him in a long time," Maria told her.

"All right," Estella said. "Do you know anyone else who would still be talking to him?"

Maria hummed as she thought. "Maybe Teddy," she said.

"Teddy?" Estella asked. "Do I know Teddy?"

"You've seen him. He hangs out at the One-Stop on Twentieth Street. Tall guy, skinny, with just a beard and no mustache."

The tune Maria had hummed worked its way into Estella's thinking. She could still hear it, high and soft, a distraction that teased at meaning. With it playing in the background of her attention, Estella could not remember anyone who looked like Maria's description. It didn't matter though.

"That's right. I know him. So, do you have his number?"

Maria giggled. "Teddy's one guy who never has a phone."

"Okay," Estella said. "Thanks."

"Stell?" Maria said. "Are you okay?"

Estella stopped herself from sighing. "Fine," she said. "No problems."

Maria paused. "Call me some time," she said. "When you're not looking for Tommy."

"I will," Estella said, but Maria had already disconnected.

#

Teddy still hung out at the tiny neighborhood deli his cousin owned, using the rarely used rear dining room as an office of sorts. He...facilitated things, Estella recalled. She ducked through the wooden bead curtain that separated the dining room from the store, stirring a faint clatter that announced her.

She heard the steady tapping of fingers on wood before she entered the room. Teddy was at a corner table, rapping out a solid beat against its top as he leafed through a dog-eared notebook. She recognized him.

"Hey, Teddy, long time," Estella said. "I'm looking for Tommy."

"Do you see him here?" Teddy asked, never breaking his beat.

Estella unzipped her coat, already overwarm. "Maria said you might know where he is."

"Stella, lovely Stella. Haven't seen you around," Teddy said with greasy charm.

She shrugged. "Been working."

Teddy smiled to himself.

"Haven't seen Tommy in about a year," he said.

Estella looked away from him. "All right," she said. "But if you do, tell him I need to talk to him."

"What for?" Teddy asked. "He wasn't any good to you."

"I know," she said. She paused, deciding how much she should tell him. How much she had to tell. Another beat, separate from Teddy's, caught her ear. She saw the metronome ticking away on the windowsill.

He followed her gaze.

"It helps," he said. "You should get one."

"Maybe," she said. "Look, Teddy, what Tommy used to go on about, the music of the stars and all that—"

"Spheres," Teddy said.

"Spheres. Right," she said. "I wanted to ask you, what do you think about it?"

Teddy cracked his knuckles and stretched his arms out in front of him. He resettled himself in his chair and resumed tapping.

"Have you ever heard of apophenia?" Teddy asked, and laughed when she shook her head. "That's what they call it when you can hear a song in some random sound that's repeated enough. Your mind makes music out of it."

"Is that what's happening?" she asked. "Is that what Tommy figured out?"

Teddy laughed again, but there was an edge to it. "Tommy didn't figure out anything."

He slapped his hand against the tabletop.

"Tommy thought he did, but he was wrong. He let the sounds in his head get to him, and then he disappeared. I don't think anyone has seen him since that happened. I think he's gone, Stella. Gone to wherever he thought the music would bring him."

"Where would that be?"

"Who knows? Could be downtown, could be Atlantis. You never know with him."

"You sound like you might believe him," she said.

Teddy stared at her for a long moment. "And you don't?"

Estella shook her head in quick denial. "Tommy lost it," she said. "There's nothing there to believe."

"Okay," he said. "If I see him, I'll tell him to find you."

She smiled and nodded. She knew she had been dismissed.

#

The night had grown colder since she entered the deli, and she pulled her coat's collar up around her ears as she walked back to her car. The air smelled of ice. The sky above her rolled like ink spilled in water, darkness swallowing the yellow light of the city. She felt it peering down at her, watching to see what she did.

When she got back home, she left a message on the voicemail at work. She wouldn't be in again tomorrow. She thought she was coming down with something. Then she pulled the shades to let in the bright night, buried herself in her blankets, and willed herself to sleep.

In the morning, she went across town to a music store and got a metronome. When she got back, she emptied out the cartons of keepsakes that filled the coat closet to find her Nonna's old wristwatch. She wound it and it ticked, relentless and unmusical. She put it on her wrist and wrapped her hand around it. It was like another pulse.

Teddy was right. It helped. The steady rhythm did not allow the other music any room to turn or grow.

The day stretched out around her. She wasn't sure what to do with herself. She revisited some of the conspiracy sites, but in daylight they seemed silly and ugly and probably loaded with viruses. She stretched out on the sofa and tried to nap. It didn't work. She realized she was waiting for something.

By midafternoon a fine, dry snow had begun to fall, sifting down like sugar over the narrow lawns and closely parked cars. She watched the snow glitter against the greying sky until it was invisible outside the cones of the streetlights. Plows rumbled by.

She started when her phone rang, buzzing in her hand. She didn't recognize the number.

"Who is this?" she said as a greeting.

"Stella, it's Maria," came the voice. "Are you okay?"

"Yeah, I was sleeping. What's up?"

"It's Tommy," Maria said.

"Did you see him?" Estella said, too quickly. "Did you tell him to call me?"

"Stella—" Maria began, but then her voice was gone in the rush of a coming storm. The sound that came through rose and fell like wind, like a whistle, trilling and rustling and full of motion.

"Hello?" Estella said, loud and frightened.

"Hello," a voice warbled back, like birdsong. "Hello, Estella, hello."

It was not Maria's voice.

"Tommy?" she cried.

A high note trailed up beyond her hearing, any words it carried stretched past meaning. The note dropped again, resolving into a cadence like speech.

"Listen," it sang. "Listen. Listen. I'll tell you what I've seen."

A burst of static cut across the sound. The signal stuttered and dropped.

"Tommy?" Estella asked again, but the phone was dead.

She could still hear the storm-song, off-kilter and wild. It was in her head. It was in the sky.

After a while of listening to its whisper and taunt, she put in her earbuds and logged into a streaming channel that played only ocean sounds. The crash of waves in her ears and the steady knock of the metronome on the table drove out the strange music and kept it at bay. She sat and watched the snow come down, afraid to sleep again.

#

In the dark of early morning, Estella tugged the buds from her ears. The ocean was not enough after all. The music had found a way to twist the metronome's steady, steady beat, changing it, altering the rhythm.

She still felt something curious waiting to get in. Waiting for a song to carry it across whatever void separated it from her. Waiting for her to listen, to hear. She sighed, and her voice was a way in.

Inside her, behind her breastbone, a trickling chime rang out like breaking glass. She froze, frightened and excited and lost. How could it be so clear through all her flesh?

It rang again, in rhythm with the beat of her heart, with the pace of her quickened breath, with the throb and pulse of the stars shining sharply above her.

She sucked in and held her breath, to bring herself to the point of stillness, where she did not make ripples in the sound that cascaded around her. There now. The stars, the moons, the travelers between, that Tommy had joined.

She could hear them, in the dark.

One Last Mile

DES CLIMBS THE slight rise to the riverside path and reaches up high, stretching her legs and her back. Her muscles slowly loosen. She walks a tight circle, shaking them out. The morning is warm and misty, the air still heavy with the river's low fog before the sun burns it clear. Her eyes are gritty and her head still a bit clouded. The wet air doesn't help.

She got out later than she wanted this morning, out of sync with the day. When the alarm began its grating complaint at six, Des had struggled to surface. She did not expect to find her husband still beside her. He had rumbled angrily as she slapped the clock into silence and rolled free of the damp, sticky sheets. Once up, it took her too long to feed the cats, too long to clean the kitchen from the night before, too long to lace on her running shoes. Even asleep upstairs her husband inhabited the entire house, crowding her with his potential presence. He stole her morning solitude, and standing in the dim morning light she feels every lost moment.

She looks at the path before her. It is empty as far as she can see, unfurling past the edge of town. She is here too late for the rush hour of dog walkers and joggers, and there is no one else moving on the path to inspire her. She resents her husband having filled the house like the taint of smoke, clinging to her. She needs the lack of him. His reality is too demanding. She shakes her head, unsatisfied. Sounds from the town filter through to her. The day has begun.

For a long while Des stands with her hands on her hips, deciding if she will run at all. If the house were empty, she would go back home and dawdle. She sighs and reaches up to smooth her frizzy dark hair back down into its ponytail. An unseen animal crashes through the brush down near the water, more immediate than the human noises. The space behind her eyes hurts. At last she pushes off, hoping to find enthusiasm as she moves.

The path is an abandoned railway bed, reclaimed, that traces the line of the river for seventy miles. The rails were torn up and sold for scrap, but the decayed wooden ties lie buried under fine grey gravel to make a trail. It was only made a few years ago, but already saplings have made inroads at the edges, and grass grows up in the middle over the long swaths beyond town. But this section of path is better travelled and still tame, a tree-lined cloister stretching through and away from tidy civilization, curving gently to the horizon. She runs it, only half aware of the scenery, unsettled. The gravel crunches and slurs under her feet, each footfall a disturbance in the dull humid morning. Nothing feels right. Des's mind drifts, worrying small domestic angers, winning arguments she never had the energy to have. She hates when he stays home. She can smell the river beside her, flat with the squatting heat and with none of the fresh sweetness she remembers from spring. Already a slick of sweat coats her back between her shoulder blades, and beads form on her upper lip. The day will be wretchedly hot again. A song hook repeats itself in her head on an endless loop to the cadence of her steps. She hates the song. She wishes she had gotten out earlier. She wishes her husband had gone to work today. She takes a pull from the water bottle she carries, knowing already that it does not hold enough to see her through.

The sun looms indistinct in the heavy air, its yellow light hazy. Latticed branches isolate her from the rest of the world. A county road parallels the path in an echo of the river, but behind the scrim of trees she is invisible to the passing cars she hears. It is a strange sensation, the busy solitude, like being behind glass. Her own breathing fills her head, ragged and thick. The feeling of separation eases as she reaches a clearing, and she stretches her arms over her head as she crosses the open field. She can see the busy road, she can see the river, she can see the houses built on stilts on the far bank. But a few yards ahead the trees loom over again, thick here where they have been left to grow as they will.

Des speeds up as she runs into their tunnel. Just under the shadow of the branches, the remains of a demolished house crouch between the path and the road. A steep, broken stone wall opposite the ruin shores up the eroded bank where the river has cut in. This is an abandoned place, lonely no matter who is on the path. She never trusts it here. She imagines things hiding here, waiting for their chance.

The light dims beneath the branches but the ground is spangled brightly where the sun scatters through the leaves. Flashes of sunlight pull at her attention, suggestive of movements in the brush. She does not turn her head. She is not sure how far she is willing to go today. She wishes there were other people on the path. Even her husband would be welcome company here, but he will not run with her. He blames her for running without him, and for his refusal. He blames her for his drinking too. He says she took the joy from him. He says she doesn't want him to be happy, that her running is a slap in the face to him, that if she cared about him she would stop. Sometimes she believes him. She feels watched. She pushes herself to run faster.

It wasn't supposed to be like this.

Another clearing becomes visible not too far ahead. The thought of the open sky eases her mood. Des slows to a walk, takes a long pull from her water bottle, wipes at her blurry eyes. The purr and rattle of late summer insects fills the air around her. Humidity presses on her skin like a wet pelt. Sweat covers her, runs down her ribs. She flaps her t-shirt to make a breeze, then gives in and takes the shirt off. Her bra is soaked through, but the air on her bare skin is a thin relief. She can see the next mile marker in the middle distance, a dark vertical line against the golden light. For a moment Des stops moving entirely, letting her shoulders slump. Behind her, hidden by the path's curve, she hears someone running toward her with long strides, sneakers scuffing the gravel. She can't judge the distance between them. So she waits, bent over with her hands on her knees, for the companionship.

It does not come. The crush of footfalls is lost in a locust buzz as it reaches her, outswelled and invisible and then suddenly past. The sound emerges distinctly again ahead of her down the path, out of sight behind the next curving stand of trees, moving away.

Des stands stiffly upright, suddenly cold, fine hairs prickling on her neck and arms. There is silence on the road she cannot see. She strains for the sound of a car, of anything normal. All she hears is the noise of the insects and the slowly receding footsteps. Tension hums along her bones. She turns on the ball of her foot and runs hard back down the path toward home.

Her heartbeat hammers in her ears. She cannot hear anything above her own thick noises. Light flickers between leaves at the periphery of her sight, disturbing her balance. A stitch burns deep into her side and she presses her knuckles against it. She fights not to slow her pace against the pain. Ahead of her, between her and the town, a figure runs on the path at her speed. It is at the far range of visual clarity in the heavy air, suggestive and undefined. She cannot tell if it is moving toward her or away. She hopes it is away. She hopes it isn't there at all.

She can't keep up her pace. Des drops into a walk, pressing her hand hard against her side. But the figure ahead of her also slows to a walk. Des stops. It stops too. Goosebumps rise on her arms. She dreads the idea of catching up to it. She looks behind her down the empty path. Haze hangs in the air, shadows and light. There is no answer there.

She forces herself to jog forward, her gait uneven until the stitch works itself out. Gradually the pain lessens and her stride grows smoother. She can no longer see the figure ahead of her. She allows herself to hope it is gone. She needs it to be gone. She wants to get home. Her face is slick and her mouth sticky, but she does not pause to drink the warm dregs in her water bottle.

As she jogs she peers back over her shoulder, afraid of what she can't see. Branches and sunlight tangle into a standing form beside the path.

She bites down on a scream, stumbles hard, regains her balance. She tells herself that it is a trick of the moving light, a curl of her hair seen wrong at the corner of her eye. She has to get home. The sounds of her footsteps and her own breathing drown any sound of the river or the road, but she still hears something heavy moving fast through the brush beside her. She forces her field of vision into a narrow slit. She does not want to see what travels with her.

The path is too long, as if it had melted and stretched in the heat. She should have been home by now. She does not recognize what should be familiar. Even the ruined house would be a marker, but all she can see are thin, glistening trees. The sun overhead is a pale blur eaten away by the misty sky. Des looks straight ahead, running hard. From behind, she hears an echo of footsteps. They may be her own. She cannot tell.

She looks back over her shoulder again. There is nothing to see, but her imagination nearly overwhelms her. She pulls herself back. She knows she is somehow to blame for this, for her fear, her exposure. Her husband has said it enough times. She wishes he were here now, the devil she knows. Blood thrums in her ears. She runs. It is all she can do. The heat-haze grows thickly into fog, crushing her view of the world into a soft cocoon to be torn through but not escaped. Against it, closer than she expects, a figure materializes and fades away.

Her chest hurts, the air too thick. There is only one way open to her. Des pushes harder, needing now to reach that other runner. It will dog her until she falls if she does not catch up. Her lips twitch into a thin smile as she thinks, it can't be worse than being alone. Finally, the distance narrows. She wipes the sweat away from her stinging eyes. She sees the figure clearly now, the dark hair pulled back, the scar on its calf from a long-ago bike accident. The figure finally pauses, turns. The face is a blank, only shadows making the suggestion of features in the empty space. This is the company she sought. It lifts its hand to her, and she meets it.

The clockwork stops, wound down to nothing. She is alone, after all.

II. New Skins

Imago

COOL AIR FLOWS down upon us. There is light there, where the wind eases in. Perhaps we can reach it today.

The way up is narrow and close. It is like sliding through a snake's burrow, under rock and leaf mould. The walls smell of damp wood and loam, but warm, as if the sun washes them. Except there is no sun here. Not this far down.

Women's voices, low and calm, float down from above us. I cannot make out the words, only the soft music of it. Terra shrugs, unconcerned. We must keep climbing.

In the corners, in between the echoes, shadows of memory seep in.

"Have we done this before?" I ask Terra, but she only looks at me slantedly over her shoulder and doesn't answer. It really makes no difference if we have done this, if we have been here already. Now is all that matters.

My arms ache against the pull of my weight. I can feel the soil between the stones and beams where it spills out under my digging fingers.

Above me I can see the dim shape of Terra's bare, dirty feet gripping any toehold to be found. She hisses when splinters break off in her hands and feet. I hiss too. The quick pain is always expected, and always a surprise. When we reach the clean cool air at the top of this pile, we will help each other dig the splinters out.

But now, we climb. The sweet voices above us spur us on. They spur me on. I cannot truly speak for Terra. Her breathing is harder than mine now, and the distance between my head and the soles of her feet is shorter than it was when we started. She was firstborn, and was always stronger. I feel the ripple of her weariness sink around me.

My cloaked shoulders itch against the rough walls of the shaft. I hope they do not tear against the splinters and spurs.

Terra stops. I hear her breath ease out in a long sigh. I reach up and cradle her foot in my hand, letting her push against me, giving her my strength beneath her. She climbs a few more feet before she stops again. My strength is not enough. She will exhaust us both.

I look up into the shadows of her long wrappings. I can see clear light around her, picked out in fragments around her small body. Fresh air cuts through the warm earthy scent of the walls. We are so close now. If Terra would only climb, I am sure the women above would reach down to help her through the opening, into the sun.

"Terra," I say. "Can you see them?"

Her face tilts toward me around her raised arm, and I think she gives me that sidelong look again. But she does not. Her eyes are white. Her mouth is slack. There is no more breath in her.

The voices above me grow quicker in their cadence, gently urging me to keep climbing. I still cannot make out their words.

I reach up and grasp Terra's thin calf, pulling her down toward me. It is the only way. She slips down against me, tight within the walls. She is so dry. Her wrappings tear. I wriggle upward, against her, until I cannot move further. She is in my arms, my sister, my other. Her face is already shriveled. I am stranded here between roots and sky with lost Terra. I press my mouth into her neck and bite deeply. Her dry skin crumbles like dead leaves beneath my teeth. I swallow. I consume. She will still travel with me.

Her bones fall past me as I strip away the flesh that binds them. At last her head tumbles free, rolling down between my full belly and the warm wall. I listen for its landing, but no sound rises.

Sound only falls. The women sing to me, calling me, wanting me to climb to them. I cannot see them yet against the blinding ring of sunlight, but they sing of how they wait for me. Fortified, I can pull my own weight up the last few yards and meet them. They will reach down for me. They will lift me free. They will help me dig the splinters from my fingers and feet.

I have done this before. I remember it now. When I reach the top, I will spread my wrinkled wings in the cool wind to dry. And then I will soar.

A Clockwork Muse

CLUMSY WITH PAIN, she is borne down by the weight of her own fractured thoughts. Light glares. Unformed, unfocused, she cannot link one perception to another. Minutiae pick her apart. She is trapped in the details, present and past transparencies overlaid to create a cloudy mass where there is no yesterday, no before, only now, and now, and now, neverending. She clings to what she can.

Eventually the pain eases, resolves itself into the stretching of her muscles, the beating of her hollow heart. Sensation, inexplicable. She believes she knows what it is. Her mind locks it into its place. There, now. It is real.

She is aware of a childhood, but she cannot hold it. The memory slips. Automata have no past. She knows she is a construct, an imitation of a life cobbled together from borrowed memories. They are all true. She remembers sitting in a field in the July sun, waiting for her mother to spread the picnic blanket. She remembers the slow ache of arthritis in her hands when she shoveled the winter's first heavy snow. She is fragmentary and erratic in her recollections but convinced of them all the same. They are in her, loose as fallen leaves, and each is real.

But she is not. Her eyes are green glass, windows into the illusion of her soul. The man standing in front of her sees what he wants in them. He has imagined her into being, shaped her and done the fine work of her machinery. What rare elements did he use to assemble her, his Galatea, his Eve: platinum wires, slick titanium joints, silicon, smooth pale lab-grown skin through which the shadow of her composite skeleton can be seen. She is breathtaking, inhuman, flesh over plastic bones. She breathes.

"Delia," he says. "Come here."

She walks gracefully, as if she had always stood erect on her narrow feet, balanced her mass against gravity's subtle pull.

His name is Stephen. She already knows it.

His hands on her shoulders, running lightly down her arms. She feels it. She trembles, gooseflesh rising, alive.

He assesses her. She stands still, unsure, expectant.

"Fine," he says. "You are fine."

Feminine, she reaches up to smooth her hair.

Szmenski steps around Stephen, leans close to her and places his hand over hers, following her motion. "Yes," he says. "You are fine." She knows his name as well. She glances at Stephen, the need to do so innate.

Stephen's mouth twitches but he stands aside to let Szmenski scrutinize her.

Her hands are restless. She picks at her nails, running her fingers around the edge of them over and again.

"Stop it," Stephen says. "You'll ruin them."

Szmenski gently pulls her fingers apart. "Relax, Delia. There is no need to fret," he says.

He guides her hands to her sides, poses her like a demure mannequin.

"You are quite talented, Stephen. Delia, thank you."

Szmenski steps back to allow Stephen close to her again. His breath moves loose strands of her dark hair. She has no sense of him.

"Thank you, Doctor," Stephen says, never looking away from her. Just past his ear Delia sees Szmenski slide open a panel and leave them to themselves. She remembers.

\#

Beside Stephen in the quiet darkness, she wonders. Synapses fire, electricity jumps the gaps, makes its circuit. She thinks time may be passing. She remembers sunrise. Her head is full of stars.

\#

He leads her to a seat before the window, positions her at an angle to the light. He tilts her chin up and away from him. She looks over her shoulder at the clear blue sky.

"Stay like that," he says, retreating across the room. He picks up paper and charcoal, sketches her outline quickly before going back to fill in details. There are many portraits of her in the house, the bulk of them with her face tilted away, as though Stephen is wary of capturing all of her.

She is curious. She lingers over the sensation of her neck extended, the pull of the muscles. Outside, leaves rustle in the wind.

There is a flicker in her memory, in her vision. She can see herself sitting there. She remembers seeing it. She feels as if she is falling. Her limbs do not match her perception. She loses her pose, turning back to Stephen with her lips parted, already asking.

"What is it now, Delia? I told you to stay still." He is angry with her. She is finite, she is lacking. She is not what he wants right now.

#

Szmenski comes and goes. Sometimes he speaks to them, genial small talk about the day that reveals nothing; other times he watches quietly from a seat in the studio as Stephen paints. Delia has the feeling that she remembers him from before, but she has no before. His presence slots in among all the other pinpoints of memory.

#

Stephen poses her again, this time standing with her hands pressed together palm to palm, fingers brushing her chin. She remembers praying, fervently. Clean tears spring up in her eyes. She does not know why. The mood fades. She dislikes modeling for Stephen, is subtly shamed by the multiple versions he makes of her. He has not yet begun this repetition, is still preparing his palette. She searches for other distractions.

There is a fine tear in her skin along the edge of her thumbnail. She picks at it until she can pinch it up and pull it back. She peels her hand like an orange. She is vaguely expecting pain, and blood, but it does not hurt. She is not surprised by the lacework of wires and slim rods revealed by her picking. She keeps going, stripping the skin from her arm in a long sleeve.

"Delia!" Stephen cries.

He reaches for her, crushing the metal bones of her hand in a hard grip as he stops her.

Without the skin to conduct sensation, she is only aware of pressure. She pulls her hand away, watching the slide and flex of her machinery.

"Don't touch anything. We have to fix this," Stephen says.

"I don't want it fixed. Not yet," she says.

"You can't stay like this," he says, already moving away.

#

She remembers leaping from the cliff's edge into the cold deep pool. She landed badly, slamming into the water's surface before it gave in to her weight and let her sink. This stings like that did, like a raw electric current across her chest and belly. She jumps away from it, fearing the drowning that will follow.

"It's okay," Szmenski says, calm as air.

The needle glints and sparkles as it threads her skin back together. There is pain, but it is not hers. Still, she flinches.

"Be still, Delia," says Szmenski.

Her body relaxes. His hands are familiar, the slow process of reconstruction has happened before. She watches his hands move across hers, the delicate stitches he leaves behind. It will heal into scars so pale they will lay like lace on her skin. Ghosts of what will be. She remembers it.

Szmenski is always the one to put her back together. He has never allowed Stephen that privilege. Sometimes he reconfigures her, changes her into something slyly different. All the iterations echo in her, dissonant and interchangeable. Memories fade and bloom. Once he had called her Adele.

#

She lies close beside Stephen as clear morning floods through the windows. She has not slept, it is not part of her. She studies him in the new light, the length of his nose, the texture of his skin, evaluating, comparing it to her own. A bird shrills outside the window and he opens his eyes at the sudden sound. From her angle she can see the glass arc of his cornea where it floats on his eye. A scrim of sunlight traces its curve. She watches the spark and scroll of data flow across it as he comes awake.

She blinks twice, reading her own scroll. She is made in his image.

"Stephen," she says. "We are the same."

He turns his head toward her, his fine hair rustling on the crisp sheets.

"No," he says, calm as an empty sky. "I am your maker."

He is peaceful, certain.

She turns away. There is no response to such a statement.

He reaches for her, brushes her hip, her belly, but she rolls away from him. The sheets are cool under her. She rises. At a distance she knows who she is, but she cannot separate herself from the tangled threads of the other lives she has impossibly lived. He did as well as he could. He is not capable of perfection. She throws open the window, grips its frame so tightly her fingers ache, closes her eyes against the sun.

Light like a downpour washes over her, through her eyelids, through her skin. She is alive, she is warm with it. She is something else than her own machinery. The facets click together, slotting into place. She is everyone within her, mosaic and whole.

"Come back to bed, Delia," Stephen says.

"No," she says. "I am leaving this."

She is surprised by his speed, how fast he leaps up and spins her away from the window.

Stephen slaps her across the face, hard and fast. Pain flickers across her skin, prickles like fragments of sulphur burning.

"You do not get to leave," he says. "I made you. You stay with me."

She lashes out like a cat, responding from some other life. His skin rips under her nails. Silver mesh glistens, revealed. There is no blood.

For a moment they are both caught up in staring at his machinery, and she remembers that he does not remember. Then he looks up at her and snarls. She feels his scentless breath on her face. She braces herself to shove him back, but he grabs her arms. She throws herself backward against the window and feels the glass splinter behind her, hears the crack of the wooden frame. The sutures at her shoulders tear loose and she is falling. Stephen clutches empty sleeves.

The air seems to hold her, for a moment. She hears Szmenski shout inside the room, but she cannot see him. She has closed her eyes. This has happened before. The sudden light is overwhelming.

Out of her skin, she is free.

In the Bright Sunlight

TOM DROVE STEADY, just over the speed limit. He imagined Claire beside him in the car as he pressed down evenly on the pedal. She had always made a game of the radio, searching until she could pull in a local talk station, searching again once the signal was lost. Now, the radio stayed off. Tom didn't care what was being broadcast.

Five hundred miles north and west of home, the landscape was familiar and still subtly different, the change too gradual to pin to a point on the map. He had not been to this country in years. He realized he had missed it. Trees rose in different abundance, the great rocks lay closer to the surface, the sun, searing in cool air, struck at a different angle.

Claire, too, became subtly different in that cool air, under that different sun. She rose very early to walk by herself along the shadowed forest roads. She often missed breakfast. Her fingers grew stained with mud and ink.

One day Claire disappeared into the quiet woods, and no search could find her. Not even a trace of her. It was as if the forest had swallowed her and all memory of her.

But Tom remembered. He knew the questions she had been asking. He suspected what she had done.

Oh, I have been

The knowledge made it harder. The first year after she was gone, he could not go back. Nor the year after. The third year he called, he made arrangements to come again, to face his loss. It was there waiting for him in the yellow and green painted cabin that backed to the trees on the south side of camp. Nothing distinguished this cabin from any of the others, except it was the last mortal space that had held Claire.

He left his bags on the step and walked up the hill behind the cabin to the road that ran between the camp and the deeper woods. The buzz of insects was loud up here, and the snap and creak of the trees.

Standing in the bright sunlight, he peered blindly into the shade of the forest. From where he stood, there was nothing to see.

#

Carl, the camp's owner, had found Claire's octavo notebook the year before, soaked in a vernal stream, still bound in dulled red leather. He had mailed it to Tom, a late and unwelcome Christmas gift. The notebook was warped and sprung, its thick pages standing open like a blown rose. In places, faded ink scrawls still remained. Tom had pressed the book under heavy boxes to try to close it, but it was too far gone for that. The pages gaped at him, veined with water stains and the spidery ghost of Claire's handwriting.

Tom did not try to read it right away. He left it on his dresser, where he could see it from his bed before he slept and when he woke. When he leaned over it to reach the mirror, he could smell the mud and dead leaf fragrance that had soaked the heavy pages. That was her scent now.

Oh, I have been

Mother is here, has fed me from her...I am one of hers now on earth as in heaven

Stars above us, I have been set below

#

Tom thought about the ugly year before she had walked into the dim forest, when they had argued again about children. He remembered how angry she was at him for even bringing it up, for being so selfish to remind her that he hadn't wanted them, that he had run down her clock.

She had hated him then, her rage a vital thing between them for weeks until it cooled. Until she had cooled. When she was finished with her rage she was no longer warm to him. He had hurt her too deeply this time. Like a fool he had thought that coming north to the camp would give them some measure of healing. She had agreed to it, so he had hoped.

He had missed her hand in his, the pressure of her body in bed beside him, for a long while before she was gone.

...under the stars, Mother, here I have been set

earth below heaven below

#

Eventually, the rest of the camp put itself to bed. Tom sat at the painted table on the cabin's screened porch with a plastic cup of Southern Comfort in his hand. His light was the only one in the camp, so late. The quiet night was broken at intervals by the low boom of boat hulls bumping their docks. There was nothing between him and the vast dark woods but screen and painted boards. He sipped at the sweet whiskey, waiting.

In the morning his back creaked like the floorboards from sleeping upright in a wooden chair. He stretched awkwardly by degrees until he could stand straight enough to walk outside. The air was pink with the promise of sunrise. He heard the distant buzz of boat motors across the lake, fishermen heading in to be ready for breakfast.

He could not shake off the sense of Claire behind him in the trees. Leaves rustled, twigs snapped, acorns dropped with small thuds to the forest floor. They were all her.

#

In the lodge dining room, Carl stood by Tom's table as he ate his breakfast. Tom looked away from the old man, out the wide window and over the lake. A hummingbird vibrated near the feeder hanging outside the window. There were already a group of children down at the boat launch below the lodge's lawn.

"Tom," Carl said. "I didn't think you'd really come."

"What else am I supposed to do?" he said.

Carl pulled out the chair opposite from Tom and lowered himself into it, favoring a bad hip.

"It changed things," Carl said.

Tom continued eating.

"Look," Carl said after a while. "It's not good for you to be here. Not for you. Not for her either."

Tom looked up at him, suddenly sharpened.

"What do you mean?"

"She changed," Carl said.

"Speak plain, Carl," Tom said, lowering his voice to a growl.

Carl looked at his hands where they rested on the table. He knotted his fingers together to keep them still.

"I saw her a couple of times after. Not much left of who she was."

"Is she alive?" Tom grated.

"Look," Carl said again. "This happens sometimes. People...change."

Tom stood up abruptly.

"We've known each other too long for this," he said. Carl kept his eyes down.

"Best you go," Carl said.

Tom pressed his lips together in a dry line. "I'm paid for the week," he said at last.

Carl shook his head, still watching his own hands. "I won't force you. But still best you go."

Carl pushed himself up then and limped to his office at the back of the dining room. Tom saw one of the waitresses peering through the window of the kitchen door. Her face was plain, with features in the cast of many of the people up here. Most folk in the area were related. Too small a population to keep many secrets. He abandoned his breakfast and left by the side door.

The kids down by the water were throwing rocks at something he couldn't see. He circled behind the lodge and went back to his cabin.

#

Despite the hour, he poured himself several fingers of whiskey and dug out Claire's notebook from where he had buried it in his duffle bag. He had bound it with a rubber band and wrapped it in a plastic bag, safe and hidden. When he opened the bag, the scent of the forest eased out. He sat down on the deep, comfortable bed in the cabin's rear room and let the book open itself on his lap. When the pages, free of constraint, had stopped moving, he lifted the book into a bar of sunlight and squinted to make out what had been written there.

been here...time slows when she follows the stars

I have been taken to her breast, again I have...

The same thoughts repeated again and again over the blossomed pages. Tom still could not puzzle them out into anything more. She had left him as thoroughly as she could.

He pressed the pages together and secured them with the rubber band. The book still bulged. He shoved it back under his clothes, out of his sight.

#

The cabin walls confined him, a reminder of what was gone. Outside them, the sun streamed down in broken beams between the thinly scattered trees in camp. Tom stood on the steps to his cabin, listening to the sounds of the world. Voices and noises drifted to him, children playing on the other side of the lodge, and the slam of the lavatory's screen door. He felt abandoned.

Tom walked up the hill again, across the dusty road and into the trees. Black squirrels scrabbled in the canopy. Deeper in, something heavy fell, cracking branches beneath it. There were no human sounds here.

Great shoulders of granite pushed up between the trees, a reminder of what carried the forest on its back. He clambered over them. The rest of the world fell away. He kept walking. If he were here, she might come.

Instead, she waited. Tom did not recognize her at first. The changes were more than he had imagined.

She stood still among the straight grey trunks, her skin mottled like fallen leaves. A bloom of lichen spread across one sharp cheek, sent tendrils down the thin line of her jaw. The tendons in her neck creaked like branches scraping in the wind as she turned her face to him.

"Claire," he said, hoping there was enough of her left to know him.

She raised her arm, banded with dry knotted vines, reaching for his face. He was a step too far away from her. Her long fingers brushed his lips. He smelled damp leaves on her skin. Before her arm could fall, he grasped her hand in his, stepped into the reach of her embrace and pressed her hand to his heart.

"Claire," he said again.

Her eyes were wet stones in her head. When she opened her mouth, only air drifted out.

Tom flinched at the sharp prick of rootlets breaking his skin, but pulled her closer. She leaned against him. So close now, her cool breath smelled like loam. He felt her fingers twining in and into his. Blood speckled his hands where she pierced him. Her mouth closed on his. He tasted dirt.

Abruptly, in spite of his want, he pulled away from her. Threading roots ripped out of his skin, stinging and drawing more blood. She remained a blank, as impassive as the trees.

Tom felt a weight build in the air, a pressure like something large moving slowly through the deep. He shivered. The air around them became milky. Tom struggled to breathe it. Claire stood still, but her outline rippled in the heavy air. He wiped his eyes with wet hands, struggling with expectation.

Then he felt it above and around him, a presence like a bead of sap that would harden to amber. It was the mother Claire sang to when she walked through the woods, the being that fed her when mortal life would not.

Claire made a sound between a hiss and a sigh, and he turned against the weight of atmospheres to face her. Her mouth was still open from their kiss. He saw moss where her tongue should have been. The sound that flowed from her was no voice but the rush of wind, of rain falling on wide lakes, of rock crumbling to dust beneath the heel of time. There was nothing of humanity in it. Tom still recognized it as a call. The cloudy air moved in currents around them. Something would answer. He knew it in his bones.

He ran before that possible maw could open between rocks and sky.

#

Carl was sitting at the painted table in the cabin's front room, waiting, when Tom stumbled out of the trees back into the thin shelter of the wooden walls.

"It's always been here. You look for it, or you leave it alone." He cracked big knuckles, settled himself differently in the chair. "My family has always left it alone. It knows us. It stays away. If any of us called it, it would come."

"You know how to call it?"

"Tom, let her go. You can't reach her anymore."

"Carl—"

"You don't want it. You don't want what Claire is now, as much as you think you do."

"Wait, let me show you," Tom said, squeezing past Carl to get to the bedroom and Claire's notebook. He brought it out and unwrapped it, opened it at random.

"Look," he said, tracing the blurred words with a finger. "She is all...Mother makes me all."

He thrust the book into the old man's hands.

"I miss her," Tom said. "I got scared, though. But if you help me... If she went, she can come back."

Carl gripped the book tightly. "You don't want Claire and her kind looking in your windows at night. She's past coming back. Not as she was. She called, she was answered. No one comes back."

He put the book on the table gently and stood. He held the screen door open for Tom.

Wind rattled the high branches behind them. Tom jumped at the sound of wood snapping, the creak and rush of a tree falling against another. Carl closed his eyes for a moment.

"It's time you go. You're not safe to have here anymore."

#

Tom started his car and steered carefully up the rutted dirt road out of camp. The deep trees stood tall but the huge sky dwarfed them all. He glanced back once at the dust raised behind him. It bloomed in a pale cloud, rising like a fountain into the wide bowl of the sky. He hunched his shoulders against those bright deeps. After two miles he regained pavement and increased his speed. He did not look back again.

Downstream

A S THEY LAY tangled together in bed in the dark, Paul ran his hand across Tamara's belly. She tensed as he traced the ridged ring of scars there, reading them like Braille. He had ignored them until now, looking away when she undressed, pretending her skin was smooth and unmarked. It was too much to hope it would last.

"When will you tell me how?" he asked, still lazily stroking her.

She flinched away, pulling the sheets around herself.

"Come on," Paul said. "You have to answer me sometime. With a scar like that there has to be a story."

Tamara sat up and switched on the bedside lamp. She kept her back to Paul, hunching her shoulders against him. Numbers on the old clock flickered, counting time.

"My sister. They took her from me," she said, her voice heavy.

Paul rolled toward her, curling himself around her hips.

"What do you mean?" he asked.

Tamara rubbed at her eyes with the heel of her hand. The gate was open. What would come through would come. "I had a vestigial, a twin."

He reached for her again, fingers seeking the rough edges.

"How...how was she, I guess, attached?" Paul said. There was a note of hunger in his voice.

She looked at him blankly.

"By the head," she said. "Essie's head and face were fused to my stomach."

"Essie?"

"Esther. They named her Esther."

Paul rolled onto his back and stared up at the ceiling.

"Wow," he said.

"We were six. They said she had finally died. But she was still alive. I knew it. How could I not? She was living off me."

Tamara's voice hitched in her throat.

"They cut her off and threw her away. But I got her out of the garbage and washed her off. Then I fed her. I let her bite me and use my blood again, like she used to. When she was strong enough, I hid her in the basement. In the slop sink."

Tamara closed her eyes against her memory. "She escaped from there."

Paul turned his head silently, to watch her.

"She dissolved, my parents said. Melted. Down the drain."

Paul held his breath.

"But I think she just got very soft in the water, so she was able to slide down the drain into the plumbing and out into the municipal system."

Tamara turned to look at Paul. Her eyes were wet, her makeup smeared.

"So she grew up in the sewers. She's not my twin anymore, she couldn't be after all this time in the dark."

#

Paul left early. He said he had to work. Tamara knew she had said too much, and she knew how it made her sound. Her therapist would suggest meds again, if he knew she was talking about Essie again. She wondered if Paul would come back.

She lay in the warm bed until grey daylight filtered through the curtains. The day stretched ahead of her, empty. She got up when her bladder was too full to ignore. The bare apartment loomed around her, its silence a distraction. Paul had broken open the quiet she had built around her loss, and filled the space with questions. She wished she hadn't told Paul anything of Essie. She wished he had just left.

She could not stop her mind from wandering, picturing her lost sister. In Tamara's imagination, Essie twined like a vine in the storm drains, her skin scaled with a graphite sheen. It was dark there, close and warm in the guts of the city. Pipes intersected and angled off, their slope pulling the water down their long bellies. Essie grew in there, in a long, wet womb. When Tamara closed her eyes she could see her sister down there, coated in a slick grey caul.

She always thought of Essie. She kept her close, but she also kept her blurred. She had learned how to leave her beneath the surface, let lost Essie drift there so Tamara could live her own life. She missed her. She wondered if Essie missed her in return, or if too much time had passed, too many changes survived to have anything left of what they had been.

She opened the curtains to let in the filtered light of an overcast sky. She wished she hadn't answered Paul, had just let the mystery of her scars loom between them. Pressure squatted behind her eyes. The air was heavy with needed rain. Tamara wanted to be out there, to escape the cloister of her apartment. She dressed in yesterday's clothes and headed for the river.

#

The park was empty this time of day, this time of year. Trees had begun to take on the rusty green of early fall. Tamara was glad for the solitude. She walked along the littered asphalt path by the river. The water lay in its bed, flat and low from lack of rain, slicked with a pale green film of algae. The air above the sluggish river was boggy and acrid.

The river bent here, and for a short stretch the curve of it created privacy. This was her place. She stepped off the path into the dusty weeds of the bank, as close to the water as she could be. She held onto a leaning tree trunk to balance herself, and looked over the green expanse at the other shore.

At her feet, a whisper. Language, intentional, familiar. Tamara looked past her braced feet to the water, searching for her sister. A glint of iridescence through the algae scrim drew her eye. She held to the tree and peered at the knotted grey roots dug into the undercut bank.

Essie hid there, in the tangle of roots and weeds at the edge of the river, her opal eyes gazing sightless at the sky. Tamara leaned closer to her sister, her feet slipping in the fine dust on the bank. Tears welled in her eyes. She had summoned her, drawn her out into the light where she didn't belong.

Essie's face was hollow around the bloodless, gaping wound of her mouth. Tiny sharp teeth spiraled all the way down her throat. Algae clung in patches like face paint. The weeds that wrapped her curled in the weak current, twisted and slowly writhed. When they lifted toward her, Tamara leapt back. The tendrils reached for her, slipping around her ankle. Not weeds. This was Essie, her body grown into a mass of filaments, her rooting limbs threaded like cancer through the water.

Tamara bit down on a scream as she backpedaled from the riverbank. As she fell backwards onto the asphalt path, the clouds broke and cold rain splashed hard on the thirsty ground. Essie's whisper was lost in the hush of the rain. Tamara clambered to her feet, peering through the downpour to see if Essie had followed her.

The bank was empty, its silt turning back to mud.

Tamara fled back to the streets, alone in the shrouding rain.

She stopped at an intersection to catch her breath, the light against her, traffic buzzing past in a heavy spray. Tamara could hear the sound of the sudden runoff gurgling below her feet as she stood over the storm grate near the corner. She knew Essie was down there, drinking in the runoff, her small gills pulsing, pulsing. Essie would follow her now.

The water running into the drain was already brown with the grime of the streets and burdened with scraps and flotsam. Nothing flowing from the streets was clean. She thought the storm drains must connect with the sewers somewhere in their tangle. A random fact floated up in her mind, that the old Roman word for the sewer is *cloaca*, and the word is still used for a bird's universal opening. Everything passes through there, excrement, urine, eggs. Their young must pass through a sewer to be born.

So it was with Essie, Tamara thought. No escaping the filth.

Tamara stood at the curb and leaned forward over the grate. Her hair hung in wet ropes around her face, a curtain from the cars on the street.

"Essie," she called down into the darkness. "Sis?"

The trickle of water passed beneath her in an echoing whisper. It was Essie's voice, pinging off slimed bricks and dripping its way to the sea.

Essie's eyes floated there in the darkness, green as opals.

Essie would stay close to her, Tamara thought. She must be curious to hear her name again after so long a silence. Tamara stepped into the gutter, bent and let her arm dangle down, not reaching, but allowing what might happen. Her fingers brushed the wet grate.

The green eyes blinked out.

#

Paul rang her bell as dusk slid into darkness, the night coming down fast with the weight of the rain. She let him in, relieved and wary, uncertain that she actually wanted him here. She looked over his shoulder toward the turn in the hall as he passed her in the doorway. The shadows were empty. She wouldn't be there.

He touched her arm, bringing her back. She blinked.

"I wondered if you would come back," she said.

"Why wouldn't I?" he asked, guileless.

Tamara gestured over her belly, waved her hands pointlessly through the air.

"Yes," he said. "That."

"I never talk about Essie," Tamara said. "It's too much, too much."

Paul took her hands to hold them still. He drew her to him.

"Have you seen anyone about this? About what your parents did to you and her?"

Tamara shook her head, quickly, hard, lying. Her hair flicked into her eyes and stung them to tears. She pulled her hand free to wipe the tears away. His breath came fast and shallow then.

"Come on," he said, tugging her toward the bedroom.

She looked up at him. His eyes were bright. It was easier to let him lead. It didn't really matter.

#

She rolled away from him when they were done.

"What do you remember of her?" Paul said, smoothing his hands over her tight back, quietly demanding her attention.

Now that she had begun to speak about Essie, it was hard to send her away again. Tamara still mourned the long days of her sister's absence. She could not live as though Essie was a phantom anymore. Paul prompted her, making sure the wound stayed open. He was hungry to hear it. The old loss still stung. But Tamara kept Essie's appearance in the river close to her heart. That, she would not speak of.

"I should never have let them take her," Tamara said, releasing her own pressure, giving him a crumb. She ran her hands through her hair.

"It wasn't your call," he said. "You had no control over it. Over any of it."

"She held on," Tamara said. Words spilled out of her, but they were all of the past, and while painful they were meaningless now. "They started to cut her loose and she bit me to stay connected. It was right, it was right of her to hold on the only way she could. We should never have been apart."

He turned her toward him in the messy sheets. She looked into his eager face, trying to find the concern that filled his voice. Her words faded. She let her eyes drift past him to the shadows in the high corners of the room.

Paul shifted his weight, leaned quickly forward and put his mouth over her scar, latching on like a suckling infant. His tongue flicked at the knots and ridges. Tamara gagged and shoved him away. She abandoned the bed and locked herself in the bathroom.

"Come on," Paul said, his words muffled through the door. "I was only—"

Tamara ignored him. She wiped his spittle off her skin with toilet paper. Paul still talked, pressed against the door. She did not listen.

Tamara touched the scar where Essie had been cut away from her, where her remora mouth had latched to Tamara's flesh, where the rings of tiny teeth had burrowed in and scraped up blood.

Essie had her own scars, but Tamara knew Essie's had twisted into a new curve as she grew, her eyes bulging and moving in her narrow skull, gills opening on her slender neck, her legs fused and her body stretched to fill the new space. Essie had adapted where Tamara had been trapped. She had moved from the sewers to the storm drains. Where water flowed, she stretched, she travelled. She followed.

Over Paul's droning, Tamara heard Essie's voice deep in the pipes, a hollow susurrus, a tapping. She leaned over the wide, stained sink, peering into the dark hole where the stopper used to be.

The old galvanized pipes screeched and pinged as they stretched. Essie knew Tamara wanted her. She heard her. She was coming. Welds popped with a dull metal sound. How could she fit through such narrow spaces? Tamara thought. How thin could she stretch? The water had made her soft, melted her bones, let her skin bloom like the tendrils of an anemone.

Deep in the drain a green light glowed, an eye, Essie's eye. She would be here, reborn from the waters, from the filth. Something new.

Tamara heard Paul moving around in the bedroom. She unlocked the bathroom door and swung it open.

It was time he met Essie in the flesh.

Underneath

THE WINTER'S COLD lasted deep into April, and the muddy snow was slow to retreat.

At last, though, it had let go, and now the sharp wind carried the scent of damp earth. Above, the sun was a white glare in a pale blue sky. Elena leaned against the door frame, squinting into the light.

She looked over the wet porch and the scattered bodies the melting snow had laid bare. Small things, wet and soft and mangled, unwanted and left by the feral cats. She prodded the corpse of a squirrel with her toe. Its fur clung to her shoe as she pulled her foot away.

She had hoped spring would bring a return, a renewal. But no birds sang in the bright still air, no living small bodies rustled among the dried stems and new shoots.

Elena shook her head as she swept the detritus of a thousand tiny lives from her porch. She remembered when her pet cats had still been alive, and would leave dead mice for her on the doorstep. One time they brought her the chipmunk that lived in the stone wall that bordered the front of the cabin, the one she had taught to take peanuts from her hand. Now only the ferals remained, skittish and predatory.

But that wasn't right, she thought. She had misremembered. Elena had not seen any cats at all over winter, or any of their neat tracks in the snow. Not for a few years now. The cats were all long gone, her pets and the wild ones as well.

Maybe the litter of small dead things was the price of some new instinct awakened by the clinging cold. Maybe they had tried to get inside, had died seeking shelter.

She was lonely. She might have welcomed them.

\#

Aaron had died three years ago now, she thought. Before the birds were gone, but after the cats. The world was getting smaller. Elena wondered what else she would outlive.

Their retreat to the vacation cabin had seemed a wise idea, years ago when the blight and its rots had begun to empty the cities. Aaron had borrowed a van and packed it with books, seeds, and hand tools, and drove them far from the thinning crowds to their familiar get-away.

It had been an idyll, at first. They had turned the wide yard into a garden, beaten back the enclosing woods, and hidden from the failing world. No one came to the other cabins in the enclave. It was only them and the cats. Once they ventured down to the tiny general store near the main road, but it was locked up and abandoned. Feeling like thieves, they broke a window and took all the packaged food they could find. Just in case.

For the first few years the ground they prepared and planted had been fertile enough. But by the time Aaron fell ill, the harvest had declined to barely enough. Elena was cautious about their diminishing stores. She foraged, with a book on edible wild plants stuck in her pocket. She learned the tastes of acorns, of wild fruits, of twining roots. She learned to live with a certain level of hunger.

The garden flourished again after Aaron had finally wasted away at the end of a cold March. She had buried what was left of him at what had once been the edge of the property, when there were such boundaries. It was as if the garden had waited for him.

#

Pale roots scrawled across the cellar walls like cobwebs. She kept away from the walls when she went down there to bring up what was left.

The vegetables and hard-shelled squash she had stored in the cellar were turning to slime, kept far past their time. She cut away the worst parts of the potatoes and onions and boiled what was left for her breakfast.

She had started her seeds a few weeks ago, early given the weather. But she was anxious for fresh food. The trays lined the southern windowsills, and delicate sprouts were pushing up and toward the light.

Every day the young plants were taller, leaning into the sun, anchored by burgeoning roots. They seemed alien to her. Hungry. Wanting. She shuddered. She had thought about them too much.

#

Despite the morning chill she brought the trays of tender seedlings out onto the damp porch. She knew there would probably be another frost before spring truly took hold, but she couldn't stand to have them in the cabin any longer, to hear them stretch and strain toward the sun. The cold frame would keep them warm enough.

The day was clear as glass, the bare trees like a lattice around her. She thought she might as well check the garden plot and start to clear it for the coming crops. She marched down the two porch steps and over the thawing ground, feeling it give beneath her boots. The stone path to the back of the house was slick with decaying leaves, and she slowed her pace as she headed for the tool shed.

As she turned the corner, she saw the tarp had slipped off the woodpile as the melting snow shifted its weight, and much of the wood was wet. She stopped short, all at once unsure of when she had last been back here. Surely she had brought in firewood only a day or two ago. Surely she would have noticed the tarp.

Maybe she had forgotten her task midway through it. She marveled at her own confusion and pushed it away. She changed course to fill the waiting cart and lug it over the rutted, softening ground to the back of the cabin. She hoped there was still enough dry wood inside for later. Then she returned to the shed for the spade, fork, and hand tools, and crossed the muddy yard to the wide garden clearing.

The fence was still in good shape, the wire still bright, the posts still straight. Last year's vines tied the gate shut though, the brown, brittle stems twined like knots through the hinges. She tugged, harder than she thought she would have to, and the dry stems crackled and broke apart. The gate dragged a furrow across the thawing earth. She smelled mud.

As she entered the garden, Elena looked more closely at the mess of bleached stems that littered the ground. Tangled among them were the small round skulls of squirrels and other rodents. She could tell by the teeth.

She mourned their deaths but moved forward. She had to make the ground ready. The dull snap of bones breaking like twigs sounded beneath her feet. Above her, the sky was nearly white.

She dug her spade into the soil. It felt too wet, like a sticky dough. A bubble of grey-green slime pushed up through the broken crust. Dark lines swirled through the curve of it, like veins beneath a membrane. She squinted at it, wondering what had caused it. Then the bubble burst in upon itself.

As if that had been a release, thin green tendrils threaded suddenly up through the cold ground, carrying bones and feathers with them. They grew as she watched, stretching toward the bright, weak sun, snaking around her boots. She jumped away from their clinging progress, surprised at how much effort it took to tear them off. She grabbed at her tools, strode out of the garden, and shut the gate behind her. She could hear the vines slithering along the ground as she headed back to the cabin.

It was her imagination, she told herself. She was hungry, and lonely. She was letting her fears get ahead of her. She struggled not to cry. If she cried, she would never stop.

She stood perfectly still for a long moment, collecting herself. She did not hear the plants growing. She would not hear them. She kept her back to the garden.

She picked up the trays of seedlings and dropped them under the cold frame. Before she closed the glass top, she bent down and pried one tiny plant from its cell. She imagined she felt its fine roots move against her palm. She closed her fingers around it to trap them in place as she walked to what was, for her, the edge of the property.

She raked away the wet black leaves that covered Aaron's grave like a dirty sheet. His unmarked stone glistened with the trails of slugs. The dark earth over him was riddled with tiny white roots, the plants they had once supported dried up and broken away. She scuffed her boot over the damp ground. Aaron was under there, feeding the new growth that would come.

She hadn't thought of it like that when she had buried him.

Kneeling, she broke the crust of the soil with a trowel and scooped out a hole for the fragile seedling. A thick liquid bubbled up from the bottom of the shallow hole, easing over the edge and seeping into the surrounding ground. It was darker than the slime in the garden, syrupy.

Elena jumped back, horrified that she had sunk the trowel blade into Aaron's remains. But it wasn't possible. It had been too long. There would be nothing of him left.

She peered into the hole. The liquid had receded like a wave from the shore, pooling at the very bottom. It smelled of decaying vegetation, not meat. She gently prodded the soil with the tip of the blade. The liquid clung in a greasy, iridescent slick on the pitted steel.

It must be the groundwater, she thought, high from the melting snow and contaminated with the sludge of last year's plants.

She dropped the single seedling into the hole. As she patted the soil down around it, she felt the earth sink beneath her hands, as if something pulled it from below.

#

The sun still shone, but Elena could not be outside any longer. She needed to eat something and calm herself. She thought there were still a few tea bags tucked away in the cabinet. She would finish clearing up the garden tomorrow.

She scraped the mud from her boots and left them with her gardening gloves on the porch. Smears still followed her into the house, inescapable. She had never gotten used to the tenacity of it, the way dirt would find a way in.

As she wiped the floor clean, she saw the mud had worked its way under her fingernails and into the seams of her hands, despite the gloves. She picked at the dirt beneath her nails. Bits of root came out with faint snaps.

Before they had fled, before the blight, she had enjoyed gardening. How long ago was that now? How long since they had fled?

As she washed her hands she felt dizzy. Her throat felt hot and swollen.

If she were getting sick she could excuse her imaginings. She could recover.

She took the small mirror from the wall and brought it to a window to examine herself.

The skin on her jaw and neck had turned a ghastly violet, as if a huge bruise had spread over her throat. Elena pressed her fingers into it. Her flesh felt soft, overripe. Skin sagged beneath her eyes, exposing the mottled grey meat beneath it. Rivulets of grey-green fluid trickled across the revealed flesh like falling tears. There was no pain, just a strange heaviness.

It had to be her imagination. She was so tired.

She placed the mirror on the sill and leaned toward it.

She tugged gently, and felt her face slip down. Loose skin slid over her eyes like a hood. She felt streams of thin liquid flow down her face, abruptly released. She felt scattered points of sharp pressure in the liquid's wake, as what had been hidden beneath the shroud of her skin pushed out like seedings, like young sprouts, reaching for the light.

Elena dug her fingers into her sliding skin and pulled, suddenly curious, suddenly eager. Her face felt like the wet, sucking earth.

She wondered what was blooming underneath.

Serpentine

BELKISE CLIMBED THE track up the side of Sorte Mountain into the shadows of the forest, far above the sprawling slums of Caracas. The sky was still a deep, radiant blue, but beneath the trees, below the high ridge, night had already fallen. The path beneath her feet was well-worn and familiar, but she stumbled in the dark. Below her, Caracas spread out in all its tattered glory, picked out by pockets of light, filling up the valley.

Tonight was the first night of the rites, of the festival. She climbed past the crowds and their revels, the noise of the drums, the tobacco smoke and fire rituals. It wasn't safe on the mountain, alone, at night. It wasn't safe in the city she left below her either. She would take her chances in wild, in the dark. The Queen would protect her.

The Queen. Maria Lionza, Yara, was all that mattered. Belkise didn't care about the rest of the gods that had attached themselves to the young goddess as the cult grew up around her. She climbed the holy mountain to search for the Queen as Yara had been before the cult surrounded her and made her strange.

Belkise wanted to know the goddess before she had been remade as Maria Lionza. She wanted to know Yara of the green eyes, who had been born royalty, warning, and sacrifice for her tribe. Yara, who was sent to the mountain to keep her safe from the prophecy that followed her. Yara, who caught the attention of the great Anaconda that swallowed her to have her. Yara, who filled the snake to bursting with water, and washed herself free. Not Mary of the Boar. Not Maria Lionza.

Belkise climbed until the beat of the drums was no louder than the pulse of blood in her ears. When she reached a clearing beside a narrow mountain stream, she drew a circle with white chalk dust and made a small fire. She lay down on the bare earth and closed her eyes. She drew in long, deep breaths, calming herself, preparing. Around her, the night moved. She wondered if, in time, the mountain would dissolve her and take her in, as it had Yara.

The night forest smelled of eucalyptus and pine, stronger than the scent of the burning tobacco she had thrown on her fire. The trees rustled and whispered, moved by wind and other unseen things. She should fear the jaguar. She should fear the gangs. But she didn't. She prayed, and the night wrapped her in its cloak and kept her safe, invisible.

Belkise opened her eyes to the dark and waited. The air around her was charged with power. She could feel it. She waited for what would happen, what must.

When she heard the great serpent slithering toward her, she sat up. Even in the thin blue light of the moon she could see the snake that glided from the underbrush was as long as a car, thick as a tree trunk, its black markings distinct on its dull olive skin. It emerged from the shadows of the forest like a ghost taking form. Such a creature should not be here, on the mountain, away from the slow rivers and swamps where it thrived. Belkise believed she had wished it here, that Yara—Queen Yara—had heard her and sent the snake to her, that Belkise might follow the Queen's own journey.

"Will you swallow me?" Belkise asked the snake. It brushed its bulk against her feet as it moved around her. Its body was cool and solid. She reached for it, letting her hand slide over its rippling skin.

But the snake did not answer her. Instead, she heard her brother Oscar come into the house and clatter around in the kitchen for something to eat.

Sorte was three hundred kilometers away from where Belkise lay in her room. The sacred places she longed to inhabit were nowhere near Caracas. She lived in the shadow of different mountains, and wished she did not.

The spell broken, Belkise got up to help her brother with supper.

#

Their house was only one of the numberless shacks that crawled in a mass up the side of El Ávila, the mountain that cradled Caracas, rising like an anthill and hiding the mountain's shape under a sheath of shoddy buildings. Oscar had found a way to survive here, casting his lot with one of the local gangs. But Belkise was lonely and restless, wanting more than this life could offer.

Her job as a cashier in the food market did not pay enough to let her leave. She did not know where she would go, even if she could. Some fled to Argentina, Colombia, Brazil. But she did not want to leave Venezuela, for all its troubles and pain. Their parents and their youngest sister were buried here, in the Eastern Cemetery. If she could, though, she would leave the dense mass of Caracas and find a secret spot in the mountains, by herself but still close to them.

After a meal of soup and bread, she went back to her bed and imagined the real mountain, holy Sorte, that she had never seen.

Her sheets needed to be washed, but she was waiting for the weekly allotment of water to come. She felt as if the dirt were creeping over her. She was too tired to move, with the grime of the city slowly dissolving into her flesh. As she fell asleep, she heard Oscar speaking quickly to someone on his phone before going out again into the night, locking the door behind him.

#

"Look at you with your new shoes," Belkise said, cleaning up from a sparse lunch. The lightness in her voice was forced. "You don't have to be afraid of anything if Rey is giving you enough for fancy clothes."

"What do you want, Belkise?" Oscar asked with a sigh, brushing crumbs off his hands.

She looked at him slantwise.

"Bring me to the statue when it gets dark. No one will be there tonight, not if we go late. And I just need to be there for a little while."

"But why at night?" he asked, knowing already that he was losing the argument.

"Because that is when things happen," Belkise said.

He shook his head at her, and changed the subject.

"You need to stop being such a dreamer and live in the real world. Rey gives me plenty of money, but what keeps me safe is that Rey likes you, Belkise," he said. "What would keep me safer is if you would be a little nicer to him. Settle down. He would be good to you."

Belkise laughed without humor.

"And if I were nice to him? Very, very nice, and we had children? It would be as good as promising them they would be orphans," she said. "He is a snake. You made your choice, joining his gang. You know he will do what he will do, no matter if I am nice to him or not."

#

She wrapped her arms around her brother's chest and held on tightly as he wove through the cluttered streets on his motorcycle. Down here in the heart of the city the sky was sliced by a web of black wires, a net to hold them in. She squeezed her eyes closed, shutting out the slums, the wires, the rest of the world. She filled her imagination with light, and the Queen. Her brother pulled off the highway onto the narrow strip between the eastbound and westbound lanes where the statue stood.

The monument to María Lionza towered over them, draped with wreaths and other tributes. Belkise looked up at the familiar figure, glad as always that the sculptor had followed Yara's description. The towering form had Yara's strong legs and belly, with her strong arms lifting a wide pelvic girdle to the sky.

How many times had she seen the statue there, when she had persuaded her brother to drive down the freeway just so they could pass it? Up close now she could see how richly this María Lionza was decorated with candles, flowers, and other offerings. The great statue was a locus for all the faithful who could not follow her to Sorte Mountain in October. Belkise had always been one of them. She could never scrape together the money to make the pilgrimage to the sacred mountain for the rituals and the blessings. What money she saved for each fall was spent on something else long before October could come.

She had been hungry all her life, it seemed, but now the familiar gnawing was erased by the flutter of nerves. She knew somehow that something would change tonight. Something.

Oscar walked his motorcycle under the line of trees a short way from the statue and parked it there, hidden from the road. Belkise did not wait for him as she walked toward the monument. She pulled a flattened cone of paper from inside her blouse and unwrapped a cluster of spidery white wildflowers.

"How did you find those?" Oscar asked, catching up to her.

Belkise blinked, slowly.

"I don't remember," she said. "Maybe in the empty lot above the house? They are for the Queen. Maybe she let me find them."

Oscar frowned at her.

"Are you okay?" he asked.

"I will be," she said.

"I wish you could go to Sorte," he said, putting his arm around her shoulders.

She sniffed at the flowers she held.

"Someday," she said. "Until then, I will meet the Queen here."

"You never used to be like this, Belkise," he said.

She did not take her eyes from the tall figure of María Lionza, who had been Yara.

"No," she said. "But I am like this now."

She stopped walking, and gently moved out from under his protective arm.

"Wait in the trees," she said. "I want to do this by myself."

Oscar raised his hands in agreement and surrender, and went back to his motorcycle.

Belkise circled the base of the statue until the spot where she stood felt right to her. She pulled a small bag holding chalk, a candle stub, and a broken cigar from her back pocket, and under the dim glow of streetlamps she began to recreate the private ritual she had imagined so many times before. She was ready for it to become real now. Before she finished drawing her circle she paused. Something already was kindling in her. She drew in a deep breath.

"Oscar!" she called over the sound of a passing car.

"What is it?" he replied from the shadows.

"As soon as I am finished here, I need to go to the river."

"Why should you go down to that filthy sewer?" Oscar asked, stepping into the yellow light. "There is nothing there for you."

"I will know something when I finish," Belkise said. "I will know how to make the water clean again."

"Ha!" Oscar said. "They have been promising to clean the Guaire for years and years. It will never happen."

"Oscar," she said. "Trust me on this."

He tossed his head, neither yes nor no, and retreated back under the trees.

#

The cigar had gone out, leaving a dark earthy taste on her tongue. The candle burned down to a pool of wax spreading across the dirt. The chalk circle was broken where her motions had smudged it. She raised her face to the sky, lifted her arms.

"My Queen," she whispered. "My Yara. I am ready."

She felt something just beyond her, a breath that brushed her cheek, a touch that almost reached her outstretched fingers, stroking the flowers she still held out. From the corner of her eye she saw motion, a tall form moving across the narrow island in the stream of the highway lanes. She closed her eyes, hoping.

Her stillness was shattered by the flat sound of a gunshot.

Belkise flinched and fell to the ground. Behind her in the same moment she heard the grunt and thud of the bullet striking a body. She knew the sound too well. What might have been was gone. Fear and a terrible certainty gripped her as she leaped up and ran back toward the trees where Oscar waited for her.

In the shadows she saw a glint of light reflected from his motorcycle, but it was not Oscar who stood beside it.

Rey leaned over Oscar's bloody body. He looked up at Belkise's harsh gasp as she saw him and caught herself up short. She stared at him.

"Why would you do this?" she asked, her voice breaking.

He smiled at her and shook his head.

"He knew why, little one," he said. "You don't need to. Go home now. We have things to finish."

She ignored him, sobbing, and stumbled forward to kneel beside her brother's broken body. She grabbed his jacket, and turned him to face the sky. Rey had shot him in the back, and the bullet had torn open his chest like a terrible blossom opening.

She still clutched the handful of white flowers she had brought for Yara. She placed them on Oscar's chest, to cover the gaping exit wound. The long petals softened, growing dark with his blood where they lay over it.

Belkise stopped crying. Something else moved her. She kissed her fingers and pressed them to the edges of the ugly hole, trying for a moment to press it closed. Then she ran her bloody fingers across her face from forehead to chin, and cheek to cheek. She looked up at Rey then and spoke a word she did not understand.

She shuddered as if the ground beneath her shook. What had touched her before had gripped her now. The soul that stirred within her was not her own. Her confusion lasted only a heartbeat before she was silenced by the new spirit.

Far in the distance, behind the mountains, thunder rumbled and purred. The air held the faint scent of rain. Belkise climbed to her feet.

"Take me to the river," she said to Rey.

He smirked at her.

"You are in no position to give me orders," he said. "You are funny now, but look at Oscar. He was funny once too."

Belkise smiled at Rey as if she owned the world.

"I am not afraid of you," she said. There was something hard in her voice that had not been there before. "We are going to the river."

Her stance and her tone made Rey shake his head in wonder at her gall. But he gestured to Oscar's motorcycle.

"All right, little queen," he said, mocking. "Get on. You can drown there when the rain comes."

She stepped forward but only to laugh at him before she darted across four lanes of blacktop toward the river, lucky that the traffic was so light, so late. Rey grabbed at her, but she was already past him.

The stink of the Rio Guaire met her before she could see the edge of the concrete trench the river ran through, neutered and channeled into submission. Beneath the sweep of the highway a fringe of trees and wild brush had found purchase in the cracked pavement, separating the constructed riverbed from the city above it. She scrambled through the overgrowth and down the cement slope to the slow-moving water.

She could hear the slap of footsteps behind her as Rey chased after her. She knew he would.

"Belkise!" Rey called to her as she started down the embankment.

"Yara," she said over her shoulder. "I am Yara."

"You're crazy," Rey said. He ran faster, slipping as he followed.

She waited for him on the edge of the retaining wall above the water. The eyes she turned to him were as green as the sea.

He raised the gun he still held but she lunged forward, punching him, tearing at his clothes, scratching at his face, too close to shoot.

"You crazy bitch!" Rey shouted, startled. "I would have let you go!"

He grabbed her roughly, tightening his arms around her, crushing the breath from her lungs. But Belkise thrashed, wild and strong. She grinned despite the pressure on her chest. She knew he lied. He struggled to keep his grip.

"Snake, you will not have me!" she cried out, twisting like a serpent herself. They fell from the wall into the low, dirty river. He fought to keep his head up, but she fought to bring him down. He could not hold her as she turned herself to face him, close as a lover, her legs entwined with his, her arms still trapped under his but her fingers busy.

She burrowed her hands beneath Rey's shirt, scraping symbols into his skin with her nails. She muttered beneath her breath, old words in a language she should not have known. And she smiled at him, as benevolent and inhuman as a saint.

"I do not belong to you," she said, and with a flex of new muscles broke his hold on her. He fell back. He swelled like a blister filling, ripping his clothes, filling his mouth so he could not scream. His skin split where she had scored it with an ancient, rippling pattern, fluid streaming out. But the pressure within him built faster than it could be released, and he burst in a flood of water and bones.

Belkise laughed, free of him and his cruelties and wants.

Thunder crashed overhead, storm clouds sweeping over the valley, swallowing the stars. Then the heavy clouds ruptured, and rain poured down, hard enough to splash up from the river's surface like stones bouncing off pavement.

She laughed again, and raised her arms to the torrential sky, dancing in the river. This is what she had been waiting for. This was what she wanted.

The water rose around her, fast and sweet and clean, as if Caracas had never been. The current lifted her off her feet, tumbled her, bore her down beneath the rushing surface. The snake that could not hold Yara had not held her either.

The last of her breath bubbled out, and she refilled her lungs with the fresh, cold water. It was good. It was right. The Queen would let her follow. She closed her eyes, reveling in the weightless surge of the current as it filled her, and spun her, and carried her out of the binding city.

Now, now after all these years, she would go to the mountain.

Chrysalis

DARK-EYED SELA SLOUCHES in her seat, leaning against the bus window, watching the world pass by through her reflection in the glass. She has a plain face made prettier by the mystery of the scene visible through it. The skin of her neck is tight and itchy, but she doesn't move to scratch. Her hands are clasped and tucked between her thighs, her shoulders pulled up as though to ward away interruption. On the crowded commuter bus she is very much alone.

The bus stops at its appointed place on a street lined with mirror-fronted office buildings. The facades create the illusion of a doubled mass of people moving before them. It is easy to be lost in such a busy place, unseen among the crowds. It is just as easy to watch unnoticed.

She moves with the flowing crowd, head tucked down in the collar of her black cloth coat, until she reaches her own mirrored building and disappears behind the glass.

#

Sela spends her day in the familiar, controlled sphere she has made for herself. She is unremarkable, pleasant and perfunctory with her colleagues, and competent in her work. She shares nothing of herself, and gives no one any reason to ask.

Her construction breaks like an egg when the young man steps up to her desk just before five o'clock.

She did not see him approach through the glass doors to the suite, although she normally catches any motion in the hall. Sela does not know this man, yet there is something familiar about him that softens her brittle skin. She lets him stand before her for a moment. She watches him from the corner of her eye as she arranges her desk for the next day.

"May I help you?" she says at last, rehearsed, neutral.

He is nervous, twitchy, as if he expects to be grabbed from behind at any time. His clothes are clean but old, mismatched and too big for him. Over them all he wears a long grey coat that hangs awkwardly from his shoulders. He looks young and lost.

"Yes," he says. "Are you ready?"

"I'm sorry, but ready for what? To leave? Yes." She turns away before he can hand her the expected pamphlet, dismissing him, curling back into her shell.

He puts his empty hands on her desk, leaning forward to be closer to her. "I know you. And I hoped you would already know me."

Sela looks up at him, uncertain, searching for what makes him seem familiar. His eyes are clear and unreadable, like fresh water. His skin is poreless and too smooth, his face too symmetrical. He does not look quite real. She studies him like a child would, wondering at him, trying to absorb everything. She rolls her chair back from the desk, making space between them.

His mouth opens slightly, as if he has more to say.

Through the glass behind him Sela sees a woman she half-recognizes, watching them intently from the common hall. When the woman notices Sela noticing her, she waves with a flick of her fingers and walks away.

Sela turns her attention back to the man, but she is distracted. His familiarity is slippery. She pulls her guard back into place.

"I don't think so," she says. "Is there anything else? You haven't even told me your name."

He shakes his head and steps away, reaching for the door handle. Sela quickly gathers her things, assuming he is leaving and freeing her to leave. She needs to leave. A pressure has been building in her chest all day, as if something were pressing up into it. But he remains there before her, rubbing his hands nervously on his legs.

"My name is Teff," he blurts. "Please. Your name is Sela. I've been looking for you. I am your own. You will need me, when you remember."

He reaches toward her, as if to make himself real, but he draws back his hand before he touches her. She tenses. She is glad of the desk between them now. There are still other people in the depths of the office, but not many, and not close.

"I don't know you. I don't need you. Please leave now."

He looks at her pleadingly. He takes a step closer, watching the expression on her face. "Try to remember. Please. It's important."

She does not sense any real threat in him, only a weird insistence she does not want to accommodate. She has given him too much of herself already. She looks at him with cool curiosity, and gestures toward the doors.

"Go," she tells him.

Teff nods, then turns from her, pushing open the glass doors and walking swiftly away. Sela watches him go, his movements reminding her of the patterns of a dance she must have seen once. She blinks, dispelling her imaginings.

She notices a faint smudge on the glass door where Teff pressed his hand to it in leaving. The print glows softly amber, like a dusting of butterfly scales. Wondering, Sela walks to the door and peers at it. It glows like something she knows, but cannot name. Gingerly, she sets her own hand over Teff's print. When she takes it away, her palm shines a pale gold as well.

Without thinking, she reaches up to scratch the back of her neck. Dry skin drifts off under her fingertips.

#

Sela's apartment is a tiny studio with narrow windows and sloppy paint on the walls. She is not sure how long she has been here. She cannot recall any apartment before this one. The furniture is sparse and worn, accumulated rather than chosen. There are no pictures to mar the white walls, no posters or photographs, no evidence that she cares for anyone or has enjoyed anything. She does own a few books, beat-up stripped paperbacks bought randomly on the street, opened and tried and discarded. There is no connection among the varied titles. She has made a void, nothing in it but herself, a place where no one can find her. She is content with it. It is her instinct.

Safely inside with the door locked, Sela examines her hands in the dirty light of the kitchenette fixture. They ache, the skin dry and too tight. Her fingers look too thin and too long. She flips off the light. She cannot tell if her palms are phosphorescent or if she imagines it. She turns the light back on. She wipes her hand across the formica top of the kitchen table, and tilts her head to catch how the light hits it at angles. There may be a sheen scraped from her skin. It may just be a dull reflection in the scattered gold specks that make up the pattern.

She hears the sounds of something being dragged down the alley behind the building. She peers out her side window, but all she can see is the wallowing night.

#

Over her solitary dinner she wonders at Teff. She has no memory of him, whatever he might insist. But he lingers, like someone she should know. In that he has succeeded. His insistence was a sort of flattery, even in its uncomfortable disruption. Despite all her efforts at invisibility, he had seen her.

She does not finish her meal. The weight in her chest leaves small room for hunger. She clears her plate into the sink and lies down. Behind her closed eyes, his face appears like light through her eyelids, becoming more familiar.

#

On the bus the next morning she dares to make eye contact with a fellow traveler. She holds her gaze for only a moment before the nakedness of it makes her turn away. She does not really want to belong in that world.

Sela is grateful to slip into the anonymity of her office. Her desk is a barrier to interaction when she bends over it to read the stack of new files waiting for her.

#

In the cafeteria at her lunch hour, Sela picks out a sandwich to bring back to her desk. She feels unwell again, her skin pinching and her belly sore. As she pays the cashier, the woman she saw yesterday in the hallway materializes beside her. Sela starts. She finishes the transaction and quickly walks away.

"Wait," the woman says. "Do you remember me?"

Sela startles at the persistent question, but keeps walking. "I need to get back," she says over her shoulder.

The other follows. "I need to talk to you about Teff."

Sela slows but does not stop. Nerves trill up her spine. "I don't know either of you. I don't remember either of you. There is nothing to talk about, unless you want to talk to security."

She reaches the bank of elevators and slaps the button for a car, forced to wait. The woman catches up to her and takes her arm. Sela flinches, but the other leans in, as near as a twin.

"Teff and I have the same things to tell you. Two sides to the story."

Sela pulls abruptly away and runs for the stairs. She is covered in sweat when she reaches her office. She considers calling for a guard to walk her out, but she doesn't know what she would say.

#

Sela wrings her hands so hard her knuckles split, showing thin seams of blood.

Her work space is in the front, and set apart, but she is sure someone must have noticed her distress. Someone may ask her about it. She feels her shell slipping.

She sits at her desk without the will to focus. Coworkers drift past, returning from lunch. Sela turns her face down and pretends to be absorbed in paperwork. She is glad she has nothing accountable to do this afternoon. She shuffles papers and opens files on her computer, appearing to work and accomplishing nothing.

#

Finally, at ten minutes to five she gathers up her things and abandons her desk for the night. She is not the only one heading out a little early, and she blends with the rest. She pretends not to see anyone else. The elevator to the lobby is surprisingly full, and unbearably slow. Her nerves hum. Her hands hurt. She feels sick, and slightly dizzy.

Sela escapes the building into a streaming crowd, wading into the tide. For the first moment she is unsteady and spun around without bearings. There are too many people, too much motion, no matter how many times she has navigated it before. She clutches her coat closed protectively, a shield against them.

As she steps from the long shadow of the building, Teff is there, separate from the teeming crowd. He takes her hand and holds her in place.

"Don't lose yourself, Sela," he says. "I have to make you understand something that concerns us both."

Sela pulls her hand out of his grasp but stays beside him. The hint of familiarity is still there, in his manner, in his strange face.

The stream of pedestrians breaks and swirls around them in their pocket of stillness. She is calmer than she should be in Teff's company. She knows that any connection she feels is imaginary, she knows all the warnings that apply, she knows she should go back into the building and protect herself. But the glimmers of recognition that he sparks in her mind outweigh her caution.

"I wonder if I may know you after all," she says.

His relief is palpable. "You do," he says.

Sela shakes her head slowly, trying to find a solid memory.

"Maybe," she says, watching him. "Do you know another woman, who works here too? She knows you."

Teff stares at her, a ghost of fear in his eyes. His mouth works for a moment without words.

"It's later than I thought," he says at last. "You must get home."

She is startled by the tone in Teff's voice. He takes her hand again. She lets him lead her to the corner, where a bus is just wheezing to a stop. Sela glances at the number and relaxes. This route runs directly past her apartment building.

The bus fills quickly. Teff finds them seats toward the back. He guides her into the row and takes the aisle seat, pressing close to Sela. She bends toward him.

"I should be afraid of you."

Teff smiles faintly.

"Probably. Since you don't remember me. But you don't need to be."

Somehow, Sela already knows Teff is no threat to her. Or she believes she knows. She is riding a strange line between trust and her carefully made isolation. Her world is shifting, and she is not sure how far she can let it go. She presses her hands between her knees, hiding them.

"Who is the woman who knows you?" she asks.

"She isn't what you think right now," he says softly. He sighs. "Neither am I. Or you."

"Do you know how to say anything plainly?" she asks.

Teff peers out the bus window as he speaks, distracted, turning his head to see past their reflections. "I am to help you, to give you strength. You will need me soon."

Sela does not understand his answer. It is sweeping, without the anchor of context. She tries to form a question that will clear the mystery he describes. She fails and sits quietly, troubled, watching him.

Night comes down as the bus traces its route, streetlights growing brighter against the shadows. With every stop, there are fewer riders. Teff studies each commuter as they disembark. Only a scattering of people board. He watches them too.

"What are you looking for?" Sela whispers.

Teff shifts his gaze to her. She realizes his eyes are grey. He keeps his voice low.

"Her, or one of her own. Maybe we should have caught a cab."

"You're still not making any sense."

Teff bends suddenly over her, close enough to kiss her. She is aware of his breath, of the scent of his clean and unlined skin. But he is focused on the street outside, on the fractured glimpses of it visible through the window. He leans across her, trying to find what first caught his attention. In a moment they have moved too far past it and he gives up, leaning back in his seat, still watching as they pass. His wariness bleeds into Sela.

"We are exposed here," he says.

"You're starting to scare me. This isn't a joke," she says. She cannot separate what she knows of him from what she imagines she knows. She has waited too long to protest. She has made a mistake.

He glances around. The few remaining riders are near the front of the bus. The empty space around them seems like a fishbowl.

"Listen to me, Sela. She has been watching you, but she wasn't sure of you until today."

Sela blinks. "How could you know something like that?"

Teff ignores her. "She is not some stranger who decided to play a joke. She is hunting you. She already knows who you are."

Sela shrinks back as far as she can from him.

"Get up," she says. "Let me out."

Teff shifts to block the aisle.

"Please, listen," he whispers. "She will be mother to a brood. Your existence threatens hers, and she will kill you if she can."

"What does that even mean?" Sela asks. She feels herself begin to tremble. She was foolish to have let this man anywhere near her. Each thought flickers across her face for him to see. She tries to push him away, but he takes her wrists gently and holds her arms down.

"Sela, stop. Be quiet," he says, and she looks at him apprehensively. "Don't draw attention to us. I'm telling you the truth. You know it. You can feel yourself changing. That's why you haven't felt right lately. Look."

Teff raises her clenched hands and tries to push up her coat sleeve. She yanks her hands back from him, hiding them again.

"You're nuts," she says, her voice threatening to become louder. "You're making this all up. Get away from me."

Teff releases her and extends his open hands to her slowly.

"Look," he says.

His palms have a faint sheen to them, as if there were a light inside his skin. She glances down at them and then away. As her eyes flicker up, she sees the bus driver watching them in the rearview mirror with unwanted attention. Sela pastes a blank expression on her face and stares at the driver in the glass, shaking her head, until the driver looks back at the road. Teff is enough of a problem without the rest of the world crashing in.

As Sela turns back, she catches something moving on the sparsely travelled street beyond the bus window, furtive and quick and gone. She catches just enough of its motion to wonder if she has seen anything at all, or is only reacting to Teff's tension.

"Sela," Teff says, distracting her even more. "The way you hide yourself. There is a reason. You live like a ghost because you've always known you must. It's your disguise."

"You don't know what I know," she says, her voice louder than she intends it. He is accurate. A dull fear sits like a stone in her chest. She has let him in too close. She has let this go too far.

"We all live like this," he says. "We have to. There's only a short time when we are not vulnerable. Let me help you."

Sela stares at him, a dim memory teasing her from the depths of her mind. She doesn't want it. She is still forming a reaction to his words when the bus stops with a lurch. Teff, unready, rocks toward her and away. She takes his lack of balance for a chance, scrambling over him into the aisle. Her purse spills across the floor with a metallic clatter. She doesn't care what the few witnesses will think as she runs from the bus into the empty street before her building. She hears the driver shout after her, but she is already on the steps, reaching for the door handle.

She opens the outer set of glass doors, but the second set is reinforced and securely locked. Sela searches her pockets for her keys, but they are gone, left behind on the bus. She leans against the wall of the cramped, badly lit foyer, pressing doorbells, hoping someone will buzz her in without questions.

She is already braced for Teff when he comes in behind her. She flinches away from him as he hands her the keys.

"Don't run again. Get us inside. She knows where we are."

Sela fumbles the door open. Teff takes hold of her shoulder, steering her past the elevator to the stairwell door and guiding her through it. The stairs smell of urine and dust. Echoes surround them as Teff shuts the door behind them.

"Let go of me," Sela says.

"Be quiet," he warns.

Sela falls silent. Her stomach churns. Her chest hurts. She cannot decide if she should fight or follow him. Teff nudges her gently up the stairs ahead of him, still gripping her coat to keep her from running. He presses close and whispers against her ear.

"I hope she thinks we're headed to your apartment. It doesn't buy us much, but it's something."

The soft sound of their footsteps fills the stairwell, covering any other noises there might be. Teff is on edge, twitching and alert. Sela watches her own feet as she climbs, pushing away the tangled thoughts rising in her mind. She wants to break free of his hands and flee back into her shell, but she knows she has lost her chance to go back, to forget. She knows there was never a chance at all.

When they finally reach the top landing, Teff stops and holds himself still, the pressure of his fingers enough to silence Sela as well. He listens for long moments before easing open the door to the roof and cautiously surveying the bleak landscape of it. Satisfied that they are still alone, he lets the door shut again.

"Sela? I'm sorry I haven't made this easier. But I have to show you now."

Sela looks up at him, her dark eyes huge in the stairwell's dim fluorescent light.

"I am your strength. I'm not going to hurt you," Teff says.

"Okay," she says. It is too late to say anything else.

He clutches the front of her shirt and tugs at it. Sela slaps him away, cursing. Teff releases his hold.

"I'm sorry," he says. "I need to know that you know. Before she finds us."

Sela stares at him in silence, scratching at the dry discomfort beneath the fabric. Then she turns away and untucks the bottom of her blouse.

She lets herself see her strange new skin.

"Oh," says Sela. "Oh."

Her abdomen is striated with the light emerging from within it, the skin stretched to translucence. A dark crease like a seam beginning to split runs the length of her belly.

And she knows. She recognizes this. Images flash through her mind, of squirming masses, and the sensation of bodies, so many of them, moving, striving. And the light. And the memories, of what she will do.

"This is what you meant," she says. Her voice cracks on the words.

"Yes," Teff says.

"Oh," she says again. "I remember now."

She draws a deep breath. "I was hidden for a long time. Long enough."

"Yes," Teff says. "Are you ready?"

She pulls her shirt back into place, and folds her long hands delicately over her abdomen.

"Yes," she says.

On her answer, Teff cracks open the door again, and the two of them slink out onto the roof. Dim reflected light filters up from the city around them. It is difficult to see anything clearly. The world feels very far away, as far as the stars above them. Sela cannot help but look up at the clear dark sky.

"Stay close, until I draw her out," Teff says, and leads Sela toward the roof's nearest edge.

From across the open expanse comes a rustling noise. She cannot see what made it. Teff freezes. Sela realizes what a beacon her skin is. She pulls her clothes tight around her, knowing she has already given them away.

Teff turns only halfway to her, unwilling to put his back to what may be there. He whispers quickly over his shoulder. "If we cannot win this, get away however you can."

And then he is moving toward the sound. Sela waits where he has left her. In the fragmented darkness, she sees Teff stop suddenly. Something flexible and winged unfurls from the shadows before him. Pale light limns its long shape. She stands, her mouth dry, ready.

"Go!" Teff shouts to her, as the sinuous thing crashes down on him.

Sela backpedals for the stairway door, afraid of what might happen when she looks away. In the bleary light she hears more than she can see, the thud and scrape of bodies hitting each other, the grunts of pain. She bumps into the door and cries out in surprise before she opens it and charges down the stairs.

Teff was the first lure. She will be the second.

Sela runs down a handful of flights before stopping on a narrow landing. She gulps in air, waiting for the expected pursuit from above. She cannot hear anything from the roof, but as her breathing quiets she hears a soft slithering below her. She holds her breath. The sound comes again, suggestive, moving up. It is not her imagination. Shadows creep up the wall ahead of what casts them, familiar but distorted by the angle of the light.

Sela darts back up the stairs, knowing she will be followed, hoping that what follows her will ignore any caution if it thinks it will catch her.

The roof is already quiet again when she reaches it.

Teff lies crumpled beneath the open sky. A swath of light streams from him like the smear of a smashed firefly, his shining blood washed across the gritty rooftop. His body looks shrunken in its own light. He is broken.

Sela surveys the roof before she kneels cautiously beside him. His coat and shirt are gone, and his torn wings are pinned uselessly under his shoulders. His belly is burst open as if he had been crushed. Her fingers slip over his skin, smoothing his wings, trying to comfort him.

"She is here. She is injured. You have to get away. Find another place."

"There was something else on the stairs."

Teff tries to sit up, but he cannot. Sela helps him, supporting his weight against her chest. They are both covered in his blood, softly shining. As it dries, it loses its light.

"It's her own," he says.

Sela glances at the door to the stairs. In the bright darkness it seems to be ajar. She doesn't know if it closed behind her.

"I think it is waiting," she says. "I would."

With Teff's weight against her, Sela struggles out of her coat. Her shoulders bulge under her torn shirt, and she takes it off as well. She squirms against the uncomfortable itching, of the pressure of her skin peeling off her back as it stretches, of the tiny dry ripping sounds it makes.

"When your wings are dry, you have to fly away from here. Find a basement, or an attic, anywhere you can hole up undisturbed."

She tenses with a sudden spark of anger that he is telling her what she already knows. He is for strength, not memory. She has remembered. She fights it down.

A hushed scraping comes from the darkness. Sela slides swiftly away from Teff and rises to her feet.

A faintly luminous figure steps out of the shadows. It is the woman, but not. She is transformed, her body become elongated and lithely inhuman. Wide wings bell around her. There are bright marks on her where Teff hurt her.

Sela twitches involuntarily, like a horse shaking off a fly. Her skin rasps like paper against itself. She can feel her back opening, muscles tearing and shifting for the new structure of her body. She flexes her muscles by instinct, working her wings free.

"We are two of a kind, Sela," the woman says.

Sela steps backward to keep her distance. She stretches her wings out, smoothing the folds, feeling their reach.

The woman sidles forward, sinuous, compelling. Sela watches her as a bird watches a snake wind toward it. The woman's belly has begun to open, the skin scraping back like lips from dry teeth, and Sela sees glimpses of softly lit shapes moving inside.

Like hers.

"Your Teff woke you to it too late. It is my time," the woman rasps.

Teff rouses at the sound of his name. "Sela," he gasps. "It's here."

A dark shape rushes from the shadows beside the door, slim wings like a cape around it, angling for Sela as she spins. So close, she sees its face is a copy of Teff's, smooth and unworn, and she shudders as she grapples with it. The speed of instinct drives her. She wrenches its shoulder and head in two directions and drops the limp body to the rooftop. It sighs, and crumples.

In that instant the woman leaps at Sela. Sela twists against nothing, unbalanced and falling. The other is as swift as a whipshot, grabbing Sela's arms, pulling her up and close. Sela wrestles against the embrace. She unfurls her wings, still damp and glistening by starlight. She beats at the air with them, struggling to keep the woman from gaining leverage. The other holds her tightly, her long hard fingers digging through Sela's transforming flesh.

Sela heaves herself suddenly sideways, strong and certain, breaking the other's grip. She leaps out of reach but holds her ground, circling toward Teff while keeping her face toward the woman.

The woman flies at her.

Sela sweeps low and meets her. They come at each other with hard nails and glittering teeth, the battle fierce in its near-silence. Shining blood spatters where skin tears.

Sela, tattered and short of breath, throws the woman off her as her attention is pulled to Teff. He no longer sits up. He no longer shines. Sela fears for him, wanting to see if he is safe.

But the woman is on her again, using Sela's distraction as another weapon. Her fingers bruise and rip, but Sela spins before the other can get a firm hold on her shredding, slippery skin. Sela locks her hands around the woman's still-soft throat and bears down. She squeezes, sobbing with unfamiliar rage, and uses her own weight to drive the woman from the air. The woman fights wildly, clawing Sela's face and chest, but Sela hangs on. Her hands are as strong as bone.

Slowly, under her terrible grip, the woman fades. The lights inside her gutter and burn out. Sela does not relax her hands until the woman's skin and blood have gone dark. Her breath tears in her throat, great barking sobs she cannot control. The pressure within her is nearly unbearable. She knows the way past it.

Sela steadies herself, and lifts the other's lightless body in her arms to hold her close, belly to belly. She feels the crawl of her own skin as it opens, sees the light she contained seep out from between their two bodies. She feels her young tear loose from their sacs within her, feels the vibrations of their jaws as they burrow through the other's unlaid brood and into the cavern of her dead body. The pressure within Sela eases, the space where her young had been already starting to close.

"Sela?" Teff says. His voice is scarcely a whisper, but the night is quiet around them.

She shakes out her wings, tucking them neatly away in the new spaces of her body. She creeps over to him, and gently maneuvers his head into her lap.

"I'm sorry," he says.

"It doesn't matter now," she says. She looks down into Teff's strained face, then up to the stars. He looks like her. He always looked like her.

Teff stares past her into the sky. His breath is heavy. Reflected stars scatter in his eyes. She sits with him as she heals and reforms. The stars move slowly as the night wears on. Sela's wounds scab over. Teff still bleeds. He will not heal.

"Where will you move them?" he manages to ask.

She strokes Teff's cheek to soothe him, but does not answer.

Dawn stains the horizon, seeping into the city. Slowly, Teff's light gutters and his skin under her fingers grows cold. He has stopped breathing by the time Sela is finally sealed within her supple new shell. She strokes his hair and his torn wings.

"I remember," she says. "I remember it all. Thank you."

She leans down to kiss him for the first and last time. Then she tears the lips from his mouth with her new jaws, and begins to consume his softening meat.

She will need her strength.

III. Gods and Monsters

Antinomia

T OM SET HIMSELF up outside a bodega, plaintively asking for help for his imagined daughter. There were people on the street. He was good with his story. Even now, he could talk them out of money. Asa and Terry loitered several storefronts down. The red sores on Terry's arms and hands made her begging a waste of time. They were the lasting marks of her first communion, and their weeping soaked through her bandages in yellow stains. No one wanted to be near that. At least she did not have the blight, with her flesh turned hard, black, and crumbling.

"Ter," Asa said into her ear. "Look who's coming."

"Wonderful," she said, and rose from her slouch against the building.

The man walking toward them was short and muscular, and carried himself like a wrestler. Terry stepped forward to meet him, motioning Asa to stay back.

"Pauly," she said.

He snorted at her. "You said you were moving on, Terry. This doesn't look like it."

Behind him, Tom was paying attention. Terry kept her eyes on Pauly. She felt a familiar pressure build inside her skull.

"We're just passing through. Not coming back."

Pauly leaned in to her, shoving his blighted fingers into her face. "Get your fucking ass out of here."

Asa reached for him but Terry raised her hand, warning him back. She pressed into Pauly and wrapped her arms around his shoulders. He flinched from the contact. Her face ran with sweat. She knew him well enough to know he was afraid of her now, afraid of her affliction. He tried to dislodge her hold on him, but she only tightened her grip. She could feel her skin heating up, knew that it was turning an ugly boiled-red by now. The few passersby steered well clear of them.

"Come on, Pauly," she breathed against his mouth. "Don't you remember the good times?"

Then her grip slipped, and she began to fall. Asa took her weight as Pauly broke free. Tom ran to help as Terry sagged to the broken pavement. Her mouth opened, and the voice that spilled out was the thick moan of wind. It had no words for her then, and ended in a hollow scream. Her muscles twitched. She opened her glassy eyes.

"Take me home," she said.

Pauly still stood there, gaping at her. Tom lifted her like a child and pushed past him.

#

When it all fell apart, Terry was ready, full of hope. She set herself up as a prophet, telling whoever would listen that she knew the way out. What, after all, is salvation if not escape?

She got the attention of people more lost than she had been, and led them into the empty suburbs where she could preach without distraction. She swore she spoke for the divine. But the first time it spoke through her, with her own mouth, her small group of sycophants fled like moths from its coming. The spasms and fever of revelation cracked her skin like brittle leather, and she bled, and she howled, and she burned. It was nothing she could have imagined.

Only Tom and Asa stayed with her, frightened and sure. They believed her and kept her safe through the pain of it. It was exactly what they had imagined.

After that, she offered no more prophecy. She would be nothing more than a vessel.

#

Tom and Asa took turns carrying her until she was steady enough to walk. She still held their arms, her head hanging, exhausted but unable to rest. When they were clear of the populated blocks, Terry stopped and sat on the curb.

"There's more coming," she said. "Can you feel it? It's like the sky is coming down on my head."

"Your skin is bad," said Asa. "Let's just get home."

She nodded and let them lead her through the crumbling streets. The slumped houses reminded her of where her parents had lived, block after block of quietly falling-down brick capes built in a booming post-war optimism. The familiarity had drawn her out here. Years ago, she had tried to go back home. The house had been boarded up with a red cross on the door and weeds spilling out of the flowerbeds. She wondered sometimes where her family had gone. She never tried to find them. Too much had happened to her for her to go back. She replaced them instead.

The house she had chosen for her band to squat in was still solid despite a leaking roof. Tom went in first to light a lamp and start a fire. Clouds had followed them back and the air was grey, cool, and unpleasantly damp. Terry trembled, worn out. Asa guided her to her favorite chair and wrapped a blanket around her. Beside the fire she dozed and almost dreamed. It was coming. It would be here soon. She opened her eyes and gazed into the flames.

Time drifted. She roused, saw Asa reading and Tom sprawled comfortably on the couch.

"I can't go back there," she said.

"Probably not," said Asa. "We'll manage it."

Light crept in around the drawn shades, dull yellow through the overcast. There was a tentative soft knock on the front door, and the three of them pricked up. Tom rose and slipped a gun from the waistband of his pants as Asa went to the door. He peered through the peephole into the distorted face of a young man. On the porch behind him was a thin girl.

He opened the door quickly. Tom stood beside him and raised the pistol.

"Please," the kid said. "We saw the smoke from the chimney. Can we come in?"

"Why would you want to do that?" Asa said.

The kid glanced over his shoulder at the girl. She was sinking into herself.

"It's weird out here today, there's something out here, in the air. I don't know what. Look, we have food."

The kid held out a thin nylon bag to Asa. "Here, take it. It's canned stuff." He didn't wait for Asa to examine it, but rushed on. "Look, at least just let Amy in, she won't be any trouble. Please."

Asa cocked an eyebrow at Tom.

The girl had the blight, not too badly. The rims of her nostrils were traced finely in black, and her earlobes were gone. She had been pretty once.

Terry materialized at Tom's shoulder, quiet as a cat in the shadows. "Let them in," she said. "What have you got besides food?"

The kid looked at Tom, and then Asa, before he let his eyes settle on Terry. "Nothing," he said. "We smoked it."

Terry smiled. "Would have brought you farther."

She turned away from them and walked carefully back into the living room. Asa stepped back to let them pass.

Terry returned to the low chair near the fire, and she motioned Amy to sit by her. The kid hovered after her.

"Who are you?" Terry asked, waving him back.

"John," he said.

"Of course. And she is Amy, you said. And you are afraid of the dark."

John shrugged, uneasy.

"There's something big out there, like a storm coming down."

Terry paused for a moment, then turned to the girl. "Do you feel it too?"

Amy shook her head and let her hair fall over her face.

"Look, she can't talk, all right?" John said. "Let me sit by her."

"Why can't she talk?" said Tom.

"Blight," John said. "Her tongue's gone."

Terry picked at her bandaged hands.

"Something gets us all," she said.

They all fell silent. The fire popped.

"We saw you in town," John said. "We saw you be overcome. It's like that for Amy too. It comes on her like that."

"Really?" said Asa from the doorway. "Just like that?"

John looked up at him, confused and wary. Terry watched him begin to figure it out, and nodded her head. Tom stepped up to John and pulled the trigger. The shot was huge in the small room, flat and ugly. Tom fired again, and John collapsed like a broken wheel.

Echoes hung over them for a few bleak seconds before Amy opened her black-stained mouth and shrieked. The girl lunged forward but Terry grabbed her and held onto her. Amy's cry fluted up from shrill to musical, and her body heaved with sobs.

"Like a bird," Terry said, wonder in her voice. "Listen to her."

Suddenly Amy convulsed, her spine crackling as she writhed. Her eyes rolled back under fluttering lids and her cries decayed to grunting. She twisted out of Terry's grasp and fell heavily to the floor. Terry stepped back, almost into the fire. Amy rolled, and her thrashing hands clawed and locked around Terry's ankle.

"Get her out of here," Terry said, kicking free.

Amy grew quiet where she lay, her breath coming in long gulps. Tom and Asa bundled her up and carried her to the back of the house.

Terry leaned over to see what was left of John. The carpet beneath him was sodden. She wouldn't look at his face.

"This next," she called out. Then it was on her.

It spoke through her as a low rumble, a darkness come like storm clouds rolling up from the horizon. Her vision filled with thick golden light, blinding her. Tom and Asa came back into the room but she couldn't see them, only their thin shadows against the sudden heavy glare. They saw the sheen in her eyes and grabbed her, held her up as her head rolled back and her legs shook and faltered. She could not hear them anymore, could barely feel their hands on her where they gripped.

Image faded into image, light into light. She saw the ghosts of everything. It was in her.

Then, like a wave, it passed. She shrugged away from Tom's lingering hold, wiped the loose spit off her mouth with the back of her hand. Her legs gave out and she sat heavily before Tom could steady her. She waved him off.

"I need water," she said. "It hurts."

"There's a pool down the block that has water in it, knee deep at least. We could use that," Asa said.

"Now," Terry said, her skin flushed red and already beginning to peel. The two men carried her across the dry ragged lawns to the lonely back yard. The pool was aboveground. Asa climbed into the tea-colored water, his feet kicking up slick leaves from the bottom. He braced himself to take her weight as Tom lifted her over the side. She was burning. Her skin shredded away under his hands, curls of it floating on the autumn air.

Tom clambered in and together they lowered her into the cold brown water. She cried out as her head began to slip under, then shut her mouth and eyes and let it take her. Under the surface she opened her mouth to let the water in, to let it cool her fire. Although she held her breath, it filled her throat with a bitter taste like tobacco. She opened her eyes then, and suddenly missed the air. Her back arched in panic.

Tom and Asa each took an arm and pulled her up to sit. They knelt beside her as she coughed and swallowed air. She wiped flecks of leaves from her stinging eyes and looked up into the steely sky.

"Let me rest," she said, slurring. Her head fell forward and she was gone.

#

She woke with a start and struggled free of the blankets wrapped tightly around her. Asa stroked her cheeks as she calmed down. She realized she was on the back porch of the house. There was still daylight. She got to her feet and held onto the bare railing.

"Where is Amy?" she said.

Asa pointed to a shrouded figure stretched on the ground.

"I don't know what happened," he said. "It looked like a fit. She stopped breathing. She never came out of it."

Terry swayed where she stood, finding her balance.

"This is bad," she said.

Asa put his arms around her.

"She had the blight. It was probably worse than it looked. We couldn't have known."

Terry pulled away from him.

"No," she said, her voice tight. "It wasn't the blight. This is bad. He spoke through her like he speaks through me. This is so bad."

She knelt next to Amy's body and tugged back the sheet. Amy's face was dark, the skin puffed and seamed like lava.

"She couldn't bear it. She was too weak," Asa said. "Not you."

"We have to leave here," Terry said. "It isn't clean here anymore."

Asa looked at her evenly.

"He follows you," he said.

Terry threw the sheet back over Amy's face and got to her feet. She could feel the pressure building behind her eyes. Her cheeks warmed, and she blotted at her mouth with the damp bandages on her wrist. "Where's Tom?"

"Over in the next block digging a grave."

"I have to see," she said, and stumbled toward the front of the house. Asa began to follow her.

"No," she said. "Stay with Amy."

Terry made her way to the street and slowly across it to the front steps of the house there. She sat down, dizzy and exhausted. Her head was full of lightning. Her skin burned from within, and she peeled off the bandages covering her hands and arms. Steam trickled from the sores. This was it now, this was her turn to carry it.

Her scalp pricked, and she squinted up to the sky. Fire rained down in threads and droplets. The air sparkled. She stood and raised her arms into it, turned her face up to the flames. Her hair smoked where the fire landed. She opened her mouth to it. She worshipped, uncertain, afraid.

Darkness stirred.

The clouds were black now, and roiled in her head. She could not see, the light would not come. Tom and Asa were gone from her. She was somewhere they could not follow. The rumble rose to a roar, the voice made of thunder and wind and the crash of waves. It was coming, through her, its promise filled. Her skin burned, scattered away like ashes. Her flesh smoldered, exposed. Her heart flinched away. She was not ready.

Afterimage

"**IT** BURNS," ABEL said, his voice rising toward tears.

Reina folded the lenses and put them in her pocket, then pulled the drapes over the wide windows and turned to comfort the boy.

"I know," she whispered against his cheek. "But it will be worth it."

With gentle hands she steered him out of the dim parlor, into the cool depths of the vast old house. Breezes followed them down the halls, the currents twining about their feet like cats. The boy sniffled, still on the verge of crying.

"They're here, aren't they?" he asked. "The angels?"

"Yes, they are," she answered softly. "Someday you will see them."

#

Her family had lived in this chill, shaded house for years, among the unrevealed angels, waiting, waiting and hoping to see.

Reina had never seen an angel. No one had, as far back as the family stories went. But her mother had promised her they were true, they were real. And in her turn, Reina had promised Abel.

#

Hot summer bloomed around them, but within the house the rooms remained dark and cool, the drafts flowing through the long, shadowed halls as fresh as early spring, teasing. Each day, when the sun was at its strongest, Reina held Abel before the parlor window and placed the lenses over his empty eye sockets until the sun's angle changed. Each day, she guided him back to his room to rest, the angels still invisible.

While Abel rested, Reina walked through her house, hoping against the experience of years to see, to see. But her eyes had been blinded by the plain world before them.

Abel was not so limited. She had made sure of that.

#

She pulled back the draperies and held the lenses up to the boy's hollow sockets again. She focused the hard yellow light into the empty spaces again. The full strength of the summer sunlight fell on him. She held his shoulders, keeping him still even as the ripe golden heat became almost too much to bear. The breezes that flowed around them were startlingly cool, unaffected by the sun that poured down.

Abel whimpered but held still.

This time, thin threads of smoke trickled out from behind the lenses, and a spark kindled in the darkness of his skull. Bright golden flames jumped and filled the space where his eyes had been. He cried out, in joy as much as fear.

"I can see!" he sang. He swiveled about, breaking free of her guiding hands, searching, seeing.

The light flared as he moved about, brighter than the sun that sparked it.

"Come here," she said, nervous of his newfound skill. "Does it hurt? You mustn't tire yourself out. This is new. You must learn how to use it."

She reached for him. His temper flared its own flame. He jumped away from her, away from her hands, her constraints.

"I won't," he said, turning his bright, bright eyes upon her. He ran into the cool shadows of the house, out of her sight. She pulled the drapes closed against the light and followed.

In the dimness she could not see well, her own vision faded from staring vainly into the sun. But it did not matter. She knew the house as well as she knew her son's face. She trailed after him, the cold drafts sliding around her legs, stirring like fog.

He would be in his room, she knew. She opened the door he had closed against her. She wondered at the draft that flowed out from behind it.

Deep in the shadows she could pick out the hot, shining embers of his new eyes. Finally. Finally. He would be able to see now.

"Abel," she whispered, her voice as cool as a winter's day, wishing him calm. "Look around us. Are they there? Can you see them?"

"Yes," he said, quiet, reverent.

He turned his bright burning eyes upon her, no longer angry.

She gasped as the light in him caught her, her own eyes charring in their sockets, her hair and dress ablaze. Ash spun off her on the rising wind pushing through the house. She could not breathe to scream. But she heard Abel's voice, sweet and soft, through the rush of the flames that consumed her.

"Angels," he breathed, as the light spilled from his empty eyes. "At last."

Summer's End

"IT'S NOT MUCH of a town," Josh said.

Dana shrugged, watching the landscape rise and fall around them as Josh sped north on Route 41. Through the windshield, late August sun fell warm across her face.

"Up here, it's all these little spread-out towns. The main businesses were the lodges, fishing, hunting, family stuff, but most of those are gone now too."

She turned to watch his profile.

"I haven't seen my mother's family for years," he said. "But it's time."

He slowed as they approached another of the tiny villages that clung to the edge of the highway.

The plain blue road sign said "Newbrook," but the mosaic of woods and fields continued. Then they passed a few widely set houses and were suddenly in the center of the town.

Dana looked around as they passed a low-slung motel set back in the trees, a small apartment block, a bank. At a T-intersection marked by a stoplight was an IGA, a dollar store, and a shuttered pizzeria. Past the light on 41 was a beer store and a medical clinic, then a few more houses on narrow strips of lawn.

Josh pulled into the driveway of a faded ranch house and turned off the engine. He sat for a moment, then reached over and squeezed Dana's hand.

"Are you ready for this?" he asked.

Dana watched the impassive front of the house. No one had come yet to greet them. Not even the curtains twitched.

"Sure," she said.

As they climbed from the car and stretched, a young woman finally came out and stood on the porch, waiting for them to climb the steps to reach her.

"Hey, Claire, you look good," Josh said. "This is Dana." He nudged her forward.

"It's nice to meet you," Dana said, and held out her hand. Claire hesitated before she took it, as if making up her mind.

"Claire and I used to play back in the swamp behind the airport when we were little," Josh said.

"Airport's been gone a long time. No one wants to fly in or out of here anymore," Claire said, looking past Dana with moony grey eyes. "Nursing home is out there now. But there's still Airport Road, and swamp."

Dana looked from Josh to Claire for any other details, but Claire kept her eyes on Josh, and Josh looked up at the curtained windows.

"Summer's almost done," Claire said. "And Dad, well..."

"Worse?" Josh said.

"Let's go in," Claire said, and ushered Dana and Josh into the entryway.

"Dad's in there," she said, gesturing toward the living room.

Dana followed the line of Claire's outstretched arm to where a man slumped in a rocking chair beside the television set. His face was slack and moist, without any expression. A blanket spread across his misshapen legs looked spotted and damp, almost moldy, and his feet jutted out at broken angles from beneath the stained cloth.

Dana took Josh's hand. "Can he hear us?" she asked him softly.

"Maybe," Claire said. She herded them out of the room again.

"Our family originally came up from Massachusetts, after the witch trials," she whispered, leaning close to Dana's cheek. Dana held still. Josh looked disgusted, but Claire ignored him. "Now the whole province is full of Masons and Mason cousins. We bred like flies. And they say there's a weakness in the blood."

Claire straightened and raised her voice. "A weakness that lingers. So I'm surprised you came back, Josh, after your mother got away."

He looked over her shoulder to where Joe drowsed. "You knew I would," he said.

#

"What's with Claire?" Dana asked him as she put her clothes into the dresser.

"She's always been a little off," Josh said. "But she's okay. I mean, she's friendly, but she will say strange things at times. You just have to ignore it."

"Did you tell her my family is from Massachusetts too?"

"No," he said.

Dana closed the drawer and stuffed her bag under the bed.

"She makes you nervous," she said.

"Yeah," he said. "Sometimes."

He made sure the door was fully closed.

"Family can do that to you," he said.

#

Dana woke before Josh did, and padded out of their room in search of coffee. The quiet in the house was broken only by cars passing on the highway.

She went into the bright kitchen and looked around. The coffeemaker had been set up already. She turned it on and leaned against the counter while she waited for the carafe to fill.

Hung above the door was a dark wooden figure. She thought it might be some rustic crucifix. She reached up and took it down from its hook and found it wasn't a cross after all. It was a damp clump of woody roots about the size of her hand, still spotted with clots of dirt, wound to form a loose nest. Two straight sticks stuck up at angles from the top of it.

Claire came out of her room and saw Dana standing there holding it.

"The Mother Root," she said, strolling into the kitchen. "The Lord of the Woods."

"Is it for good luck?" Dana asked.

Claire smiled and moved past her. "Sure," she said. "Something like that."

#

In the afternoon, Josh and Claire went out together. Dana stayed behind, not sure if she had wanted to. She drifted around the house, avoiding the living room where Joe sat in his slow decay. He disturbed her, not for his infirmity but because she had a primitive feeling that his helplessness was a lie.

She slipped on her shoes and headed out the kitchen door and around to the front of the house. The car was gone. She followed the road, and kicked rocks along the pavement for a few hundred yards until the asphalt sidewalk began. The sun fell hot on her head and back, and drove her shadow ahead of her. There were a few people about, mainly going in and out of the supermarket driveway.

She reached the intersection in front of the IGA, and crossed the road to the wooden barn that was Davey's Variety Store. The front was decorated with inflatable toys and two soda machines. She went in. It was warmer inside than she expected, and smelled of lumber.

Beside the front door was a small cooler with tubs of worms for sale. Behind the counter, a man Dana assumed was Davey sat reading a magazine, an oxygen tank clicking beside him. His skin was pale, almost grey, and his hair clung damply to his forehead. He did not look well. He glanced up at her as she came in then looked back down.

She checked out the bandanas and sunglasses and fishing supplies, the beach toys and the bin of old DVDs for sale. The store was deeper than she had thought it was, with rooms separated by arched doorways. She kept poking. In the back, past the bookshelves loaded with used paperbacks and the pegboard displays of toiletries and children's clothing, was a door labeled *Private*.

Dana looked toward the register, but shelves blocked her view. The only sound in the place came from a radio set on a shelf somewhere toward the front.

Curious, Dana turned the knob, and was surprised to find the door unlocked. She opened it to find a narrow hall and a staircase to an upper floor. Layers of footprints smeared the treads in dust. At the top of the staircase was another door, poorly fitted in its frame. Light slipped out in slices along its edges. She climbed toward it, drawn by the yellow light.

The door opened silently when she tried it. She stood for a long time on the threshold, taking in the contents of the room.

A pile of dry vines and flaking grey mud leaned in a tangle against the far wall, crowned with a small, unnervingly female figure. Dana stepped quietly across the room, plucked the figure from its nest, turned it in her hands.

It was carved of a greasy white stone, about ten inches tall, with rows of heavy breasts like animal teats and a grossly swollen belly. The face was a swirl of scratches, and from the forehead two horns curved up in a semicircle. The figure's back and lower half were a mass of looping tendrils.

The stone was biting cold in her hand but she held it against the pain, studying the curves and lines that turned like a Möbius strip across the oval space where a face should have been. She could not focus on the pattern. It shifted under her gaze. Uncomfortable, Dana put the figure back and tucked her hand underneath her arm to warm it again.

She turned away from the vines and the idol and examined a shelf of books that stood below the room's single window. The languages of the titles eluded her. She pulled out a massive folio, studying the dark leather cover embossed with vines and beasts. It was spongy and warm. She didn't want to open it.

She slid the heavy volume back and pulled out the one beside it. This one was beautiful, an octavo bound in stained, deep-yellow silk with a winding silver pattern embroidered on the cover. She ran her fingers over the threads, and pulled them quickly away. Something in the design had slithered under her touch.

Wary now but drawn in, she opened the book and leafed through the heavy pages. Tucked between the leaves near the beginning was a sheet of common lined notepaper covered in sharp blue lettering.

C.M. trans. Polyglot Lat. and Arab., some Grk., Germ.?.–Lord of the Wood, Black Goat of the Wood, Mother of the Wood and the Stars, Black Goat with a thousand young–incantation? Ever Their praises, and abundance to the Black Goat of the Woods. Iä! Shub-Niggurath! Black Goat of the Woods with a Thousand Young!

Without thinking, she folded the sheet and put it in her pocket.

She flipped more pages. The words on the page shimmered and turned, unreadable. She blinked, clapped the book shut, and replaced it on the shelf. Still, her hand lingered on it. She wanted it. She pulled it out again and slid it into her purse.

She looked around, suddenly furtive. The sun cut through the window above her in a wide golden beam, catching in her eyes, making her wince. The room seemed to close around her. Something could see her here. She knew it under her skin

She stepped to the door, and listened only a moment before pattering fast down the stairs. At the bottom the world filled with the thin radio music again, and Davey gave no sign of having seen her as she fled.

#

Days melted into days. Josh and Claire were often out, catching up. They did not ask her to come. Without them, Dana kept to the house. The town was too empty for her to want to wander alone.

She spent her hours reading in the living room with the husk of Joe for company. He deteriorated slowly, like a great wet cake sinking in on itself. Sometimes he sighed, but otherwise he made no sound. As far as Dana could tell, Joe never left the living room. She didn't want to be near him, but felt safer if she could watch him.

She finished the novel she had brought with her, and the magazines she found in the house. One afternoon she pulled out the yellow silk book from where she had hidden it in her empty duffle bag under the bed.

She settled back in the living room and paged through it slowly, then got out the sheet of notebook paper. She tried to match it to a passage, but the language in the book was nothing she could grasp. She read the translation over, softly, aloud, her lips bending over the stranger syllables, her tongue halting at the sounds.

"Lord of the Wood, Black Goat of the Wood, Mother of the Wood and the Stars, Black Goat with a thousand young—Ever Their praises, and abundance to the Black Goat of the Woods. Iä! Shub-Niggurath! Iä! Shub-Niggurath—"

Joe moaned and leaned toward her, reaching. The hand he raised looked eaten away, the skin grey and peeling. Dana shrieked and leapt up, the book falling from her lap.

Claire stood in the doorway. She smiled, her lips wet.

"It's all right," Claire said. "Don't let him bother you."

"He doesn't," Dana said, gathering herself again.

"Josh, I mean," Claire said. She went to smooth the blanket over Joe's misshapen lap, pressing him back into the chair. "There now," she said to him.

She came over to stand beside Dana. She glanced down at the book on the floor, then up into Dana's eyes. "Josh knows what he has to do, and he doesn't want to do it. Family is hard sometimes."

She lifted Dana's hand in her own, turned it over.

"Look," Claire said, pressing her finger against Dana's palm. "Do you see what's written there?"

"No," Dana said, pulling her hand back.

Joe snorted wetly in his chair, falling to one side. Claire moved to straighten him.

"I think you will," Claire said, bending to tend her father.

#

The evening was warm and still. Dana had talked Josh into leaving the house with her, to show her the quiet town. He had grown up here, after all. There were only six streets, and most of the small houses that lined them were dark.

"The way you talked, I always thought Newbrook was bigger," she said as they looped past the nursing home back to the main road. "There's nobody here."

Josh smiled. "There are some," he said. "The town clears out after tourist season. But twenty, thirty years ago, we lost a lot of people. They went...elsewhere."

"I guess that happens to a lot of small towns. The economy changes and it's hard to stay."

"Things do change," Josh said, and fell silent.

They strolled past Davey's, and Dana laughed with sudden bravado.

"You know there's some weird shrine in there?" she said, keeping her voice low.

Josh stared at her, no humor in his eyes. He stopped walking.

"What do you mean?" he asked.

Dana looked at him.

"Above the shop. Upstairs, there's a shrine set up. Fertility goddess, I think. And a collection of old occult books. I couldn't read them. Someone had started to translate them and-"

"Why were you upstairs at all?" Josh hissed at her. "Did anyone see you?"

She stepped back.

"I was just goofing around."

"What is wrong with you?"

Dana blinked back sudden tears. She looked at her feet, then up over Josh's shoulder at the side of Davey's building. The narrow attic window was lit with a dim yellow glow. Shadows moved across the light. She wondered who was up there.

"I'm sorry," she said.

He pushed past her. "We have to go home now," he said.

He was sweating. She realized he was scared.

She followed him into the soft blue night, back up the road.

#

She heard him leave the house before dawn. She heard low voices from outside, then the crush of gravel under wheels. She rolled over and willed herself back to sleep.

Claire woke her before noon, standing over her, watching until Dana opened her eyes.

"I haven't been a good host," Claire said. "I've left you to your own devices all this time."

Dana blinked and sat up on the edge of the bed. She was groggy and pliant, beginning to feel unmoored in this empty town.

"It's all right," she said. "I've found stuff to do."

Claire sat beside her, her grey eyes huge. Dana could feel the heat from Claire's skin.

"Where's Josh?"

"Around," Claire said. "But I have something for you."

Dana opened the twist of paper Claire handed her. Inside lay a tangled clutch of roots, black with fresh mud.

Claire grinned. Dana nodded, closing her fingers around it.

"This is the welcome you should have," Claire said. "You do belong here."

"I hope so," Dana said.

#

The afternoon was almost gone when Dana realized Josh had not returned. She had lounged away the time outside in the warm, heavy air, too tired to read. Not a single car had passed. She felt as if she were waiting at the end of the world.

Claire walked out of the stand of trees that edged the property and waved.

"Dana," Claire said, "I have something else for you."

"Okay," Dana said, not moving from her seat on the porch.

"No, come with me," Claire said, coming closer.

"It's already late. Josh has to be back soon."

"Maybe. We'll leave him a note," Claire said, pulling a crumpled ball of notebook paper from her front pocket. She smoothed it out on the hood of the car and tucked it under the wiper blade.

"He'll know what to do," she said.

Dana sighed and got up, following Claire across the yard. As she passed the car, she glanced at the scrap of paper. The writing on it was the same lettering as in the yellow silk book.

#

The sun slanted down behind the trees as the afternoon waned, the sky warming to the color of honey. They walked into town, and then turned down Airport Road to follow its long loop. When they reached the nursing home, Claire pulled Dana across the facility's parking lot toward the woods behind it.

As they passed the building, Dana saw a line of slack figures propped in wheelchairs, drowsing in the deepening shade. Their postures reminded her of how Joe sagged, boneless yet waiting. From where she stood it looked as if their skin was sloughing off like birch bark, peeling away and drifting across the concrete pad in shreds. She wiped the back of her hand across her eyes.

"What's wrong with them?" she asked Claire.

Claire paid no attention to the nursing home patients. "Inbreeding. Cousins," she said, without glancing toward them.

Dana looked at the people in the chairs. Maybe Claire was right, and it was an ineffable weakness in the blood.

"Mason cousins?" she asked.

"Come on," Claire said. "It's not far."

Behind the home's parking lot, a path snaked back through rough grass toward the trees. Claire tugged Dana along behind her, urging her to speed up, to reach the woods. Cedar and pine and birch grew over the path, blocking their line of sight, forcing them to push through the branches. Over their own noises Dana heard voices, and the sounds of other passage all around. Claire gave no sign she heard anything.

In less than a mile the trees thinned out, becoming sparse and unhealthy. The ground grew soggy underfoot as they walked into the swamp. Claire stopped before they reached standing water.

"Here," she said, and pointed. "This."

The hulk of an ancient willow listed like a shipwreck a hundred feet from where they stood, rotten and broken but still alive. Where its roots had pulled free of the ground, a great pit opened, greasy with mud. It gaped like a mortal wound to the earth.

Claire raised her arm and the sky suddenly dulled, the golden light fading into ocher and purple and acid green. Night swarmed down.

Dana saw movement near the jagged pit. Long branches whipped with no wind to drive them. Distorted figures moved through shadows. Across the shallow water voices rose and fell in ugly song.

"Iä! Iä! Shub-Niggurath! Lord and mother, hear us. Lord of the woods, hear us. Shub-Niggurath! Black Goat of the Woods with a Thousand Young!"

Dana recognized the words, and screamed. She turned to run but Claire grabbed a fistful of her hair and dragged her forward into the water. "No," she hissed, her grey eyes like lanterns. "You belong here."

Dana twisted, caught. Figures emerged from the cavern beneath the willow, moving to form a ring around them.

"Iä! Shub-Niggurath! Black Goat of the Woods with a Thousand Young," Claire chanted with them, and yanked Dana's head in time to the incantation.

Dana could see the approaching figures had heads and arms and swollen bellies, but a swarm of churning limbs where legs should grow. They had faces, with the skin grey and loose and slipping. As they drew closer, she thought one was Joe. She screamed again, helpless, wild. Claire called out again, laughing.

The dimmed sky erupted in roiling black clouds, and withering cold washed over them. Water crackled and froze around them, crunching beneath the moving forms. Dana fell forward into the swamp, leaving a clutch of her hair in Claire's grasp. She struggled to rise, but the ground seemed to shift under her. She looked up.

Something had heard the chanting.

Shadows in the sky coalesced into a column of black mist, shot with lightning and scored with flickering tendrils of smoke and muscle. It descended, wet with a slime like an afterbirth. It pooled in the hole beneath the shivering tree. Smoke and ichor dripped over the figures as they called out Where the dripping touched them, they burned.

The chants howled into a frenzy. Claire had forgotten her, staring up at the blackness with joy and terror in her face. Dana gazed at the thing descending. She did not want to run now.

"Iä!" she whispered. "Shub-Niggurath!"

She belonged.

A human figure emerged from the woods, dressed in a horned goat's skull and a still-wet skin, dancing and lurching and raising its bare arms to the thing in the sky.

Dana recognized Josh beneath the costume. He chanted too, raising his voice to be heard above the roar of the tentacled cloud squatting over them, above the relentless chanting of the circling crowd. But his words were different than theirs. She stood unsteadily and reached for him, trying to answer.

Lightning cracked across the sky. Dana's senses wobbled as if she tumbled under waves.

She could see through Josh's eyes, under the edge of the skull. She watched his bare feet cross the rutted swamp to the fallen willow. She felt the weight of the dead skin hanging from his shoulders. She felt the fear that weighed in his lungs, and the need. He knew what to do.

Then she stuttered back, fell, and was in herself again as Claire lifted her and led her into the pit. There she pushed Dana to her knees in the cold mud, muttered an unintelligible string of sounds, and retreated.

Something squirmed in the slime Dana knelt in. She arched away, startled. Long flexing limbs slipped out and wrapped her body, binding her to an icy mass that moved over her skin, languid, lithe, slippery as water. There was foulness in its touch, a stirring of desires that should not be sated. The mass seeped into her flesh, displacing her. She cried out in mortal fear and delight. She wanted this.

Josh stumbled forward under his heavy wrappings, tangling with all her new limbs. She felt the crack of his head striking rock, felt flailing strands stretch from her and sink into him. He pressed in against the slick resistance of her swarming muscle, blooming as the undertow of her swelling body bore him deeper into her. He dissolved like sugar in water.

She opened her mouth to sing out but another flowed in. Great ropy strands within her swelled, filling her, bursting her apart. Her flesh stretched and shredded, her mind scattered like dust. A million icy stars spilled out of her, a million cilia thrashed from her skin into blackest space. She rose in the column of her own wet flesh and smoke, seeing across the voids through a million lenses.

The chanting voices were so far away, the creatures that made their pleas so very small. She could not understand what they said with their small voices. What they wanted. But it didn't matter.

As she opened into the cloud and chaos, she saw the vast sweep of the sky above her, as deep as time, as empty. And the million scattered stars she birthed were still too few to dispel the dark.

Strange Bodies

STRANGE BODIES WASHED up on the beach that summer. Those who ventured close could see the long white forms were not fish. They had scales and hands, fins and wild hair that grew like manes down their narrow backs. The latest priest came down from the village to anoint their cold dead faces with oil before the men weighted them with stones and threw them back to the sea. It was the way it had always been done.

#

It was a cool summer, and a rainy one. The sky was often grey, the sea winds chilly. Peter went down to the beach every morning to walk among the rocks, and to see what the waves had cast up overnight and left abandoned. If he saw a white form on the sand, he left it for others to find. Their rites were not his purpose.

Instead he filled his pockets and bag with polished stones, rare unbroken shells, scratched and dulled bottles that still held their shapes. He carried them back up the hill to his faded house and set them out like figurines on a shelf. Once there was a necklace, silver with opal cabochons, only one of its jewels dislodged by the busy water. That he wore always, hidden by his collar. He told himself it was his wedding gift to Sarah, for giving him such a fine child, but he knew he lied.

#

You are ours, weak voices said from the waves. Peter stood at the edge of the sea and looked into the grey waters. The waves turned like curving glass. He could not see through them. He wondered if the voices were real, or if he only wished them.

Peter had dreamed of those voices many times, enough that he half-believed they were memories and not his imagination. The voices made him remember things, shadows and light that might be true. They made him think of his mother, whom he had never known. His father had not even kept a picture of her, no mementos at all. He only said sometimes that Peter reminded him of her, although he would not say how.

He only told Peter to avoid the sea when the white bodies washed in.

#

When his father died, his warnings faded, and Peter followed the tides as he would even when the bodies came. He still thought of all the holidays when he was a child, when the families here had gathered in one house or another at the new year to share another set of myths about mothers and children, about other sacrifices and returns, the parables behind his father's flat cautions. He imagined it still went on like that, the stories passed on year after year, sons and daughters taking their warnings and learning their duties. Since his father died, he stayed away from that community. He knew what he knew.

He was bent over at the waterline with a twist of wet rope in his hands when a pale body sliced through the glassy water at the edge of his sight. He stepped back, quick fear in his throat. Then he recognized what she was.

He held his breath as she swam up the beach on the slick of a breaking wave. She was as familiar as his own skin, the colour of pearls, sunless, sinuous, her pale hair growing down between her shoulders and tangled with weeds. He reached out his hand to her and she took it, her own hand slender and bony. It flexed within his grip.

She was beautiful as the eel is beautiful, as the serpent is. She had teeth like an eel. Peter knelt in the surf for her and she twined her long elastic legs with his, and she sang to him with a reedy, comforting voice.

When he woke, his oiled coat was soaked through and he was numb from the cold sand beneath him. The tide had gone out, and the grey water was empty.

#

Peter believed he courted her across the long, chilly summer days. She came when he called her the name he believed he had given her: Nomi,

Nomi, Nomi. Whispered, it sounded like waves raking sand, the sound he imagined her skin made as she slid over the sand to reach him.

Once he reached out for her face and she slashed at him with her sharp eel-teeth to remind him what he owed, and his hand had slowly bled a watery pink fluid until the lips of the wound sealed together.

#

Sarah stood with him at the waterline. She tried to take his hand, but he pulled it away from her, careful of the bandage. She looked at the dirty wrappings, and at Peter's eyes. She did not ask him what had happened.

"There's another," Peter said, pointing to a pale shape in the surf.

Sarah crossed herself, unaware she did it. "Is it coming in?" she said, leaning against his arm. He shrugged her off, intent on what the sea would bring him.

The body rolled in the waves, limp as an empty dress. Peter walked into the water and lifted a sagging arm into the air. He pulled on it, bringing the head and neck out of the water. The skin was still unmarked by scavengers. He didn't know this one, though the open opal eyes were like Nomi's.

Up on the beach, the baby began to cry, a thin wail torn away by the wind. Sarah looked over her shoulder at their daughter, knew she was safe in her blankets.

"Shall I run for Father Tom?" Sarah called to him over the sound of the waves. He looked up at her. Sarah's eyes were calm. For a moment, he hated her.

"We don't need him," he said. "The sea will keep her."

#

Sarah sat in the rough grass beside Peter as he sorted his collection. The baby slept beside her, swaddled against the cool air. The salt wind pushed Sarah's hair back from her face, and she squinted up at the far, misty sun. Metal clinked as Peter dropped green coins into a pile. She turned at the small noise.

"Father Tom's sermon today was about false idols," she said, "and how we risk our souls to have too much faith in the fancies of the sea. He said our people have been tied to the sea so long we believe it is our mother, and we forget our father."

"I don't know why you go there," Peter said, his voice level. Sarah did not respond. "What else did he say?" he asked.

"He said he's writing a history of us," Sarah said, scraping her heels in the turf to expose the sand beneath. "He saw how thin the records are. He wants to complete them if he can. He's talked to most of us about it."

"A real scholar," Peter said.

Sarah did not catch his tone. "Oh, they don't like him. Father Henry was never this much of a bother," she said. "My father says it will be interesting if he can do it."

"If he can," Peter echoed.

#

He dreamed of her. He dreamed he swam out into the wide sea, although he could not swim, that his pants and cloak billowed and filled with salt water and carried him on. *You are ours*, they sang. Nomi and her kin swirled around him like a dance of serpents, until she reached for him, took him in a cold embrace. He felt like a child against her, and clung to her in sudden fear of the sea. She smiled with her eel teeth before she put her chill lips against his ear. *Breathe*, she murmured, and slipped with him beneath the waves.

#

Peter climbed the hill up to his house, a cold wind at his back. As he reached his yard he saw Father Tom leaning in his doorway, his coat pulled around him, trying to escape the wind. Peter walked up to the old man and dropped his bag beside the door.

"I've come to talk to you," Father Tom said. "Sarah might have mentioned it. You're one of the last. For the history."

He did not want to let the priest into his house, but he opened the door and stood aside to let Tom enter before him. It was only politeness to let a man get out of the wind.

Peter fed the stove to make a little warmth. It was a strange, cold summer. He could not remember one like it. He set the pot on the stove. "I'll make us tea," he said.

The priest settled himself in a chair and pulled a ledger from his pocket. He was less concerned with politeness than Peter was.

"Who was your father, boy?" Father Tom asked without waiting, his pen poised to record Peter's answers.

"Peter Kannet, same as me."

"And is he still living?"

"My father's been dead three years, sir," Peter said, his eyes cast properly down.

"How did he die, boy? Did he drown?"

"No, sir. Plague. And I never knew my mother."

"Is her family still about?"

"No, sir. She was from away. My father met her wandering, or so he told me."

The priest scratched down the details, then paused to read over the page. He turned back a few pages, scanned them, looked up again.

"This was not your father's first marriage, then. There is a record of another, a Mary Andrems."

"I wouldn't know, sir. It was long before me."

"Andrems, like your Sarah."

"Probably the same. People don't move off from here much. Or come."

The priest looked at Peter where he stood by the stove.

"That has some romance to it, but the truth is it leads to unhealthy traditions."

Peter smiled thinly at the old man.

"That's really why you came, then, isn't it? Not for our immortal souls."

Peter stepped close to the priest where he sat, letting his closeness make a threat.

"You came to see the bodies in the water."

Father Tom stood up abruptly, forcing Peter to step back.

"I came to see the bodies," he said. "That's true."

Tom flipped through the ledger as he stood there, holding his ground. He traced a passage with his finger, nodded to himself.

"Here, tell me what you think of this. Local history has it that the white bodies wash up here every few decades, every generation or two. As if this shore is a sacred place in a long migration, and not all survive the journey. The landsmen always weigh them down and send them back to their sea. It's only right."

He closed the ledger and tucked it back deep into a pocket.

"Who told you that pap?" Peter said.

"Your Sarah, among others. People talk, given time," Tom said. "Do you believe it? And the rest, like your families did?"

Peter looked past him to the small dirty window that faced the sea.

"Doesn't matter what I believe," he said.

#

Peter went to the beach as the tide slid in. The sky was heavy with possible rain and the air too sharp for summer. White skin flickered like light in the water.

"Nomi," he called. He liked to think she listened for him, and responded. Better that she loved him than that she had trained him to seek her out.

A pale shape drifted under the surface, pulled by the incoming tide. He waded in to reach it, to see if it was her, dead like the others.

"Nomi?" he called again. The dim light tricked his eyes. Did she drift or did she float?

As he came close, the shape turned in a tight circle and disappeared into deeper water. He knew what she had come for. The memory of it was real, if nothing else was.

#

"Father Tom says it's a sin, that we've let too much go," Sarah said. She clutched at her skirts, lifting them out of the surf. The sky above them hung dark. A storm was coming fast on the rising wind.

Peter put his arm around her, trying to keep her calm. He wished they had talked plainly before now. Sarah knew, in the same way he knew. He only wished he had said it aloud.

"It's no sin," he said. "It's older than his sin, so it can't be. This is what our fathers did. And our mothers."

He steered her back up onto the sand. Suddenly he did not like the sea at his back. It held too much it never showed. He made himself be stern.

"The priest has to scare you to turn you away from this," he said. "If what he preaches is true, he wouldn't need fear to convince you."

She kept her eyes turned down, tilted her face away from him.

"Do you remember her?" Sarah asked suddenly. Her voice was caught in the wind, thin as a phantom.

Peter thought before he answered her.

"Sometimes," he said. "I think I do. But I can't always tell if I remember her or the other stories."

Sarah nodded slowly.

"I think that's how it's always been," she said. For a moment she leaned against him before she stood straight.

"Let's be done with it," she said.

He kissed her sharp cheekbone, already beginning to miss her.

"Who has our girl?" he asked her.

"My sister," Sarah said. She turned to face him. "After this, Anne will have the baby baptized."

"That priest doesn't know what he thinks he does, with his history and family lines," Peter said, with brief anger that she kept hanging onto it. He did not want the possibility of another option. Not now, on the last day of summer, when Sarah knew what was expected, when they were already waiting, when time had run down. "Now, are you willing or not?"

"I am," she said. Her voice was steady.

Peter held her close for a long moment, absorbing some of her warmth. He watched the sea through her blowing hair. Nothing white moved in the waves.

"And I," he said at last, and held her away from him. Then he drew the long knife he had at his belt, slid it into the sand between them as a wave washed up, pulled it free and held it up to show her. His father, Sarah's father, every man born here, had told him what was needed, Peter thought. He did not think he had dreamed this.

"Sarah," he said, and she lifted her chin as she took the knife from him. Her hands trembled slightly, and she clasped them together around the handle, holding it at her waist.

"It's sharp as I can make it," he said. "Wait, one second."

Peter took the silver necklace from under his collar and flung it into the sea.

Sarah's eyes followed its shining arc and its splash into the waves. Then she drove the wet blade up under his ribs, setting it deep, driving grains of sand and salt water into the wound. He grunted at the heavy pain, and reached for his belly. She grabbed at his hands as the blood pulsed out, to keep him from pulling the blade free. His blood was pale, a thin red as if it had been watered down.

Peter broke her grip and staggered past her, wading up to his knees in the grey surf. He stumbled, falling into the water, still holding his head above it. His blood made a red slick in the rising waves, then swirled away to nothing. They would smell it in the water. He hoped they would follow it. He hoped they would accept him.

"Nomi!" he coughed into the wind. His voice was weak. He called again, and thought he saw her long white body slicing up from the deep water. Then there were many white bodies in the choppy waves, and many opal faces lifted to see him. Any might be Nomi, or none. He fell forward and recovered, wiped at his eyes and called her name again.

The storm broke with a single flash of lightning and a sudden steady rain. The sea was pocked with it. The pale faces sank away, invisible beneath the dark, rough water.

"Nomi!" he cried again. The breath caught in his throat. It tasted of salt.

She came then, shrouded in a breaking wave, slithering up to him in tightening circles with a hunter's patience. She watched him with her wide, unblinking eyes, and she might have smiled. He tried to reach for her, but she turned like a fish and was gone.

Peter pulled himself almost upright and looked around him in the empty water for her white body. Rain clouded his eyes. He looked up the beach, saw the shadow of Sarah still on the sand, huddled in her coat against the storm. He wanted to go back to her where she waited at the waterline, but a susurrus behind him turned him again toward the open sea. He grew dizzy. The voices were blurred in the rain, but still they whispered, *You are ours*. He did not have the strength to turn back again, but he would not have to. They would have him.

Still

I SHOULD HAVE died a hundred years ago, a thousand. More years ago even than that, I'm sure, with the stars spinning by on their wheel so many times I've lost count. The world awakened me when it found I'd left it again, another form shed. And then it birthed me anew, unwilling.

#

My father led our tribe for many years, and his father before him, and his father before him as tradition demanded. But my father had no sons that lived, and so it came to be that I led our tribe when he died. There was some complaint at the change in tradition, but I was well-enough supported and well-enough liked that the grumbling soon quieted. Life went on much as it ever had, except a woman led. It was not as large a change as it seemed at first. But a change does not need to be large to be a threat.

I did not ask for anything different, nothing more or less that we had always done. We still built our houses on the slope above the river. We still tended our gardens and hunted the sheep, and deer, and antelope. We still gathered stores against the long barren winter. We still believed our priests could speak with the gods for us, to plead our case and offer our gratitude.

I put out of my mind that the priests still had their sons to think of.

In my fourth year as leader, our fortunes turned. Spring began, and as suddenly stopped. A great storm blew through and turned the world cold again. Buds froze on the branches. Animals died in their nests.

We struggled. The cold spring lasted, dissolving into a chill, wet summer. Not even the oldest of us could remember such cold lasting as it did. We starved, slowly. I led hunts. I foraged with my people. I ate less than my due, that they would have a little more.

We starved, but we did not die. We survived the barren summer, the lean fall, the damp and muddy winter that followed.

It was not enough.

When the next spring came, the gods of the sky told the priests that a woman could no longer lead the tribe. I did not believe them. But my people did. They looked at me now as if in wonder of how I could have led them at all. They chose to forget that I had suffered with them.

They let the priests confine me to my house while prayers were said and preparations made. I would be a sacrifice, to show the gods they would be worthy of mercy in the year to come.

For a full day and night they prayed and sang, danced and burned herbs outside my door. To escape the drone of their voices I slept. Alone in my house, I dreamed of a voice like the whine of a wolf, like the yip of a fox. It rose and fell and told me that soon no women would lead us, and then no one at all. We would be set aside like old memories.

On the second morning they allowed my eldest sister, Ayedene, to enter and bid me goodbye. We had grown apart in our adulthood, but she claimed the right of kinship in order to see me. The priests would not deny that, not with our people watching and hoping for the gods to be kind.

As we knelt together on the rug, Ayedene pulled a tiny, leaf-wrapped packet from her belt. She unwrapped it and handed me the flat oval stone it contained.

"You tried, Damina," Ayedene said. "I cannot stop this, but I will do what I can to steer it. I will miss you."

I looked at the stone. It was a fleck of pink quartz the size of a fingernail, its luster dulled by the delicate figures painted on it.

"It is a charm, to help in what will come. Keep it under your tongue until you must swallow it."

She squeezed my hands between hers. I pressed my forehead to hers. We did not cry. I put the stone in my mouth and nodded. She smiled at me without joy, and left me to my end. Or so I believed.

My people buried me high above the village. They covered my mouth with cloth to still my screams, and bound my arms and legs with leather cords to still my thrashing. They dug my hole deep, to still me. They covered me with a flat-faced boulder and scratched my image into it. They gave me huge, round eyes to watch over them with, and a mouth full of sharp teeth to defend them with.

I screamed for a long time, until the dirt sifted through the cloth, down into my lungs, and I could make no sound at all. Then I swallowed the stone. The charm. And I was still.

#

At first I could not see through the new eyes my people had given me. I lay in pain, crushed and blind and mute beneath the stone that took my place in the world. All I could do was listen.

I heard the people as they came each day to pay tribute to me as an ancestor, calling me She Who Watches Over Us, erasing my name. The priests encouraged their devotion to me as a sort of house spirit, a grandmother to keep the wolves at bay, erasing my life.

The people came to the hill and worshipped me, laying gifts before my stone face. They brought flowers and cakes and honey, small dolls and jars of paint. They sang out what they carried, sang out for my blessings.

I had no blessings for them. I did not want to be worshipped.

Ayedene came each night to pray to the gods of the earth instead. She prayed for them to help me, to let me be at peace if I could not be with my people. She came for twenty-one nights, kneeling above me and begging the gods' favor. I could not call out to her to stop, to let me be what I would be. My mouth was filled with dirt. I could only listen to her droning prayers, and hope they would go unanswered.

But Ayedene was faithful, and persistent. And at last the gods of the earth listened, and agreed to do what she had asked of them. I was not asked what I might want.

When my sister went back to her house on the twenty-first night, the gods of the earth fulfilled her prayers. They eased away my flesh with sand and dust, remade my bones with minerals, bent my arms into bands of quartz around the carved stone that marked my grave. They gave me the only peace they could.

When Ayedene came the next night, she knew I had changed. My sharp-toothed mouth was bent in a smile for her. Ayedene greeted me, and told me I was an Old One now, kin of the gods, part of the earth, beyond all the tangle of mortal lives. Now I truly would see, and watch.

But the priests still had their sons to think of. They might promote me as a guardian spirit, but they could not allow the people to turn me into a savior. They had killed me once, but it was not enough for them.

They had changed me, but not diminished me. Not in the way they had hoped to. They did not know I would be changed again.

So it was no surprise when the priests' sons came in the deep of the night, drunk on sweet wine and their own bravado. They knew they were their fathers' successors, and that I was only a joke now, a silly bit of the past. I was only She Who Watches, not She Who Leads.

They pissed on my new stone face, and decorated me with old vines and rotten scraps. They laughed, and they mocked, and they came so close to me, pretending to hump the rough stone of me like dogs, pretending to kiss my sharp smile.

Then they screamed like rabbits when I reached out and embraced them with my new arms, and wheezed into ugly silence as I bore them slowly down into the earth with me. They knew fear then, as I had. But they were not so fortunate as I. They did not know how to breathe inside the earth.

In the morning, my people found their blood and skins around me like a skirt.

After that, my people brought me meat.

The priests were too afraid of what I had become to try to dislodge me or break me into bits, as much as they wanted to. Instead they declared that the people must stay away from me, that Ayedene had worked a curse to kill their sons out of jealousy and pride, using her influence as my sister to turn me against them. She was kept alone in her house for three days, starved and bound, until they buried her at the base of the hill, under my watchful eyes.

She was afraid for a little while before she died. But her fear passed, as did her breath. She is truly dead, as I should have been. I will not call the other gods to ease her. Death is ease enough.

#

My people dwindled in their valley, over how many years I cannot tell. They forgot me, and I slept, unaware and dreamless.

But I was not as forgotten as I had hoped. When another people came to drive them away, they remembered me clearly, and I woke at the noise of their complaints and pleas for my help. It hurt to come back. High on my hill I remained She Who Watches, awake but bound still in stone. The others built a dam across the river and flooded the lands that had always been ours. They forced my people to flee to strange lands and leave me behind. The waters did not rise high enough to touch me, but they obscured me from the newcomers, and in time my pain eased and I slept again.

Now they are all dead, the newcomers, my people, my gods. No one remains who remembers the gods of the earth, or the sky, or the sea. No one remembers me, as woman or as god. That is good. It is easy to die, if it is only once. But to die and return, to go through the pain of both death and birth, again, again, again, world without end—I would rather be forgotten.

And I was, until another new people found this place, found me and dragged me back with their curious hands. They pulled away the dead vines and saplings that hid me, and approached me with shreds of old stories they do not have the experience to understand. They speak of me as if their patchwork of half-heard tales were the truth, waking me again into this narrow world with its absent gods.

They don't even know what they have done. They don't know how they resurrect me when I have been forgotten, how they wrest me from peace, careless as children. They can't see me here, or hear me.

But I can see them.

Looking out through these stone eyes is like looking through a film of dust. Like looking up through moving water. Even to open them is a sacrifice. My sacrifice.

I should have been dead so very long ago.

Unless this stone body is destroyed, there will always be some new people to replace the old, who will find me when I have been once more left to sleep, to die away. They will be curious and hurtful. They will always be ignorant of what they are capable of. What they have done to me, time and time again.

But when they touch me again, they will know.

Winterking

S NOW DRIFTED DOWN on the still backs of the geese in the river. The birds sat like statuary in the thin fog rising from the water, impervious to the weather as the snow came down, and came down, and came down. The air was thick with it. Carolyn's hair was frosted heavy white as she stood on the riverbank, watching the geese, her cheeks pinched red in the cold. She had left her coat behind. She told Serge she needed to be cold to keep away the phantom that wanted her warmth. Sometimes Serge tried to stop her from going out, but he hadn't this time. Her ungloved fingers stung. At last she turned away from the muttering river and went back to the house.

Serge watched her climb the rise of the lawn. He opened the door when she reached it, and brushed the snow from her head as she came in. She drifted past him without a word, and he pulled the door closed against the bitter air. It was only December, with winter hardly begun. It would get worse.

#

One dusk at the end of autumn she had come into the house rattled and pale. The late afternoon sky filled the rooms with thick grey light. She drew the shades in the living room against the coming darkness and huddled in the shelter of lamplight.

"There is something down there," she said into her clenched hands.

Serge put down his cup of coffee and went to her.

"Where?" he said. "The river?"

She nodded.

"In the water," she said. "It wanted me to come into the water."

"Wait here," he said.

Serge grabbed his jacket as he went out the back door and across the sloping lawn toward the river. The gravel road at the bottom of the property was empty in both directions. The river was grey as stones and showed nothing but ripples around the broken branches of a drowned tree. He walked upstream toward the bridge. There was nothing to see. He knew there would be nothing. She had seen things before.

#

She was always caught unawares by what she saw, the menace sudden and unexpected even as she tried to explain its workings to him. They developed a rhythm around her visions and fears. Serge turned the heat down in the house and risked the pipes and Carolyn agreed to stay inside. Still, he checked for her every morning and often shepherded her away from the river. She could not stay away from the river and what was hidden there. She said it called her, but called her less when she was cold. It could not see her clearly then. She drew him illustrations of her struggle captioned with a language she couldn't read. Over time it became they, the threat expanding like the bloom of a red tide. She exhausted him.

As soon as he could, Serge found her a doctor, and pulled her barefoot from the cold to see him. She fought, then tolerated, then complied. After a few weeks she no longer spoke of needing the cold, no longer cowered against what waited for her in the river. Dr. Pirrone told him that the meds were working, that she was stabilizing. Serge hoped.

#

Then she called him, frightened, from Pirrone's office in the city.

"I can't come home now," she breathed into the phone. "They know where I am. They know where you are."

"Wait there," he said. "I'm coming."

"Be careful," she said, and hung up.

As he navigated the end of the rush-hour traffic, he realized what a mistake it had been to let her take the train in. She had seemed strong enough, and calm. He wanted to believe she was ready for it. Guilt picked away at his edges. They must have seen this at her appointment. Why hadn't anyone called him?

Serge double-parked in front of the glass tower where Dr. Pirrone had his office. He didn't see Carolyn. He threw on the hazard lights and jumped out. The wind, funneled down the street's canyon, hit him like a slap. Through the huge plate windows he could see the empty lobby. He looked up and down the street, throttling down his fear.

Then she rushed out from behind an outcropping of the facade. Her hair was a disaster, the wind in it, in her clothes. She did not try to hold her coat, let it flap like wings around her, let her scarf swirl up like a flag. Her eyes glittered, fevered.

"They know where I am!" she cried out. A man in all black turned to see her. Serge took her arm.

"Get in the car."

She complied, stiff and nervous.

"We're not doing this again," he said.

She was silent for the drive. He reached for her hand, but it was like gripping a clutch of twigs. He still held it all the way home.

#

The deep cold settled down. The river stilled beneath it, a field of white under the thin snow. Only the water under the bridge was free, moving in sluggish dark ripples beneath the curved span. Even the geese were gone.

Carolyn grew restless as the winter hardened its hold. She refused to go back to Dr. Pirrone. She hadn't liked him anyway, she said. She hated the meds. Serge worked from home as much as he could, staving off family leave as long as possible. He could not leave her alone for too long. Her need wore on him.

#

"The portal is sealed until winter ends," she said.

Serge looked up from the report on his screen, his concentration ruptured. "What are you talking about?"

"See the arch of the bridge?" Carolyn pointed out the wide living room window. "When the river is free it reflects, it makes an eye through which we can see across all time."

She breathed on the glass to frost it, and scratched a figure into the ice.

He came up behind her, cautious.

"What is that?" he said. "You scribble it everywhere."

She bent her head down, let her hair cover her eyes.

"I don't know. It came to me."

#

On New Year's Day she disappeared while Serge was in the shower. He came out of the bathroom to a house too still, too empty for her to be anywhere in it. His wet hair froze to his neck as he ran down to the river, yelling for her to answer him.

He found her by the bridge, squatting under the abutment where the bank sloped down into the dark river.

"He wanted me to come," she said. He, now. No longer they.

"Who wanted you?" he said. "Who is calling you?"

She could not answer. She only traced the familiar figure over and over against the palm of her hand.

"Please," Serge said, taking her chilly hands in his to still them. "I love you. You're scaring me. Let me help you."

She took her hands away from him, picked a rock out of the hard dirt and threw it into the water.

"You can't," she said. "I thought I had more time."

#

As they lay together in bed that night, she told him that she had to go, and that he could not follow. He lay awake for a long time after she fell asleep, looking into the answerless dark. In the morning she was gone, her space in the bed cold.

He did not want to believe it at first, calling for her through the house. Then he saw her coat was gone, and her shoes. He was surprised she had taken them. There were mingled footprints in the frost on the path, already dissolving in the morning sun. Someone had come up. She had left in company.

As he retreated back into the house he saw the sign scratched into the front door. How long had it been there? He looked out at the empty river. The town behind him was quiet this time of the morning. He felt watched. He scraped his fingers over the broken paint to peel away the curved lines. He couldn't read it, but he knew it was not safe to leave it. It called to something.

#

Serge waited for her to come back without any expectation that she would. He did not enjoy the sense of relief her absence allowed, as if he were disloyal to be free of the constant fear for her. Her presence still lingered in the house like a pall. To dispel it he packed up her possessions neatly, labeling each box with the precision of a draftsman, ready for her if she wanted them. If she came home.

#

By mid-February the snow had almost melted away, and the air smelled of wet earth underneath the chill. The sky was grey, naked. Even in the shelter of the house, Serge felt exposed. He had begun noticing motions at the corner of his eye, and the dull suspicion of being paced by something faster than he could run. He turned the heat up to seventy-five and left it there.

One day at sundown he went to the back door to look out at the river, drawn to it. She was there at the bottom of the yard, with tall shadows behind her that she did not cast. He could see her lips moving. *Come out, Serge,* she said. *I can see you,* she said.

"Go away," he said through the glass. She laughed. She faded into the dusk.

#

She haunted him even though he did not see her. Once he gave in and went down to the river, missing her, but the sense of something waiting to drop on his neck was so heavy he did not go back. It followed him back, relentless. His work suffered. He made arrangements to transfer out of state. He made an appointment to see Dr. Pirrone.

"She was mad," Pirrone said. Serge started at the blunt assessment.

"I know I'm not supposed to say that, but the only other way to explain Carolyn would be to say she could see God. Neither is really correct."

"But what about the treatment plan, the dose adjustments?" Serge said, his voice trailing off, losing hope.

"I couldn't help her," Pirrone said. "There was something else there."

#

Serge left the office with the wind at his back, and let it blow him down a side street away from the dwindling five o'clock crowds. He found a pedestrian cut-through and was alone almost immediately. He didn't recognize the street. Water trickled in the gutters with hollow music. The sky between the high buildings deepened toward nightfall. His skin prickled with the old sense of being watched.

Movement caught his attention. He saw her walking on the other side of the street, part of a black-clad pack. She cut her eyes toward him. He caught the quirk of her lips as she moved past. He kept his face forward and kept moving. He wished she hadn't seen him. He hoped she believed he hadn't seen her. He turned, trying to double back to the main avenue.

She was suddenly at his shoulder, her breath cold against his ear. "Serge," she whispered, and he started and turned. She was pale and as beautiful as he had wished. Ice crystals glittered through her hair.

"How have you been?" Carolyn said. Her voice had an edge of anger.

He stepped back from her. She leaned in. The cloth of her jacket rasped on his coat.

"Did you miss me?" she said.

He glanced at her companions where they stood. He thought they watched him, but he could not make out their faces. When he turned his head they resolved into a flock of shadows, tangled in the streetlights. Carolyn shifted to fill his field of vision.

He took her shoulders and pushed her back. Her jacket felt empty beneath his hands. She frightened him, but he held on.

"I never thought I would see you again," he said. "You left me."

She smiled, a sliver of ice.

"Not forever," she said. "He lets me go, sometimes."

He knew he had lost his chance.

She slid her arms around him. Her cold was unbearable. Serge tried to force her away from him but it was like pushing into water. She gave way and he only sank. At the edges of his vision he could see the shadows pouring in, filling in the lighted spaces.

"You are so warm," she said, and pressed her mouth over his. Breath flowed out of him. He felt his lungs crackle and freeze, cold like a burn radiating from his chest. His eyes grew foggy. All he could see was static and snow, spiraling into a familiar shape. He could read it now.

The Grave of Angels

CORRA MARTIN, LAST child of her family line, insisted that I bring her home as a condition of our marriage.

And home, for Corra, would always be Holyoke where it stood on the high cliffs above the sea, exposed beneath the wide murky sky. The town had been all but deserted for years now, as all the coastal towns were. But she had been away for years, and longed for it. I had no deep roots, and wondered at her insistence.

Once we reached its crumbling outskirts I understood. Her family was woven into the fabric of this town. Streets were named for the Martins, and the businesses on them as well. Martin Hardware, Martin Dry Cleaners, Martin Street Market. All of them were shuttered though, the influence of her family as diminished as the town itself.

No one went to the seaside anymore.

But we did. Corra was dying, and it was her wish. She wanted to be buried with her family. As we drove over the long, broken two-lane road that stretched across the lowland marshes toward the rising hills, Corra kept up a steady chatter of anecdotes and half-slipped memories.

Her mother had been the last living sibling of three, Corra rambled, and the only one to marry and have children. Her father was a mystery to her, unmentioned and unrecorded. Corra had had a brother once, but she believed he had died in infancy. She never knew him. She thought he might be buried here. Her mother was, in the family crypt. Her uncles, dead before she was born, had left and never come home. How much of what she told me was objectively true, she couldn't be certain. But she told me her history as she had learned it.

As we drove I watched her pinched, animated face. It was luck that I had even met her. But it was also luck that nurtured the disease in her lungs, stealing her breath and wasting her away. Sometimes she said it felt like something twisting inside her, coring her out. She had become almost

Victorian under her illness's weight, washed out and slender to the point of consumption. Yet her will to return to Holyoke was strong.

Corra stopped talking as we turned onto the long driveway to the house, her concentration at once and entirely on the property.

I wondered how what she remembered compared to what we saw. The family home was a large, plain two-story affair, with faded blue vinyl siding and sagging gutters. Its lawn had become overgrown and brown, the driveway encroached by weeds and sand. Shaggy boxwood and yew shrubbery hid the lower parts of the wide front windows. The house breathed emptiness.

I pulled up in front of the garage. Corra got out of the car and jogged up the front steps. As I followed her, I could see a light burning on the porch, dim in the daylight.

I was surprised the old house still had power. A note pinned to the front door read in wide block letters: *Generator on below. Cellar doors open for air. A.G.*

Corra pulled the paper free of its pin, crumpling it without thinking. She shoved it in her pocket as she reached for her keys.

"Who is A.G.?" I asked.

"Anna Gorney," she said, distracted, as if she thought I should have known. As she struggled to turn the stiff lock, she explained.

"Another old family in Holyoke, the Gorneys. They have always helped us."

And then with a sudden click she unlocked the door and went in without me.

#

I carried our bags in while Corra wandered through the house. Her footsteps sounded from above me as she moved through the upstairs rooms. From the entrance way I could see into the living and dining rooms. They were clean but shrunken with oversized furniture. Family photos hung on most of the walls. I went into the living room to examine one of Corra, very young, with a woman who was probably her grandmother. The shape of their faces showed their kinship.

I turned away. There was nothing else of particular interest. This was a house much like I'd grown up in, comfortable but drab. I paused to consider the blank black window of the television screen. It had been years since anything had been broadcast. I didn't really miss the content. I missed the community.

As I stood there reminiscing, I heard the low thrum of the generator in the basement. Cutting across the steady sound, though, was a scraping noise like rocks sliding across each other. I found the cellar door in the kitchen and made my way down.

As I descended the painted wooden steps, I expected to find a finished space, a playroom or a den. But Corra's cellar was dug out of the cliff's raw rock, rough, brown and layered. The floor had been leveled with painted cement. Part of one wall exposed a vein of black basalt in the native rock, honeycombed with what looked like burst air bubbles. The holes were full of shadows in the overhead light and glistened with damp. The grating sound seemed to come from the holes, but the noise faded as I leaned in to listen.

Then any subtler sound was drowned by a deep, hollow booming from far beneath me. I started, before I realized it was probably the sea clanging in some half-submerged cave. These cliffs were riddled with caves worn out of the rocks. I wondered how long it would take the sea to tear them down.

My mind was too busy. I went back upstairs to find my wife.

#

We settled in.

On the days she felt strong, Corra showed me the town as she remembered it. The first time, before we turned back home, she brought me to the edge of the overgrown cemetery where her family had built a small chapel over the family tomb. It was hardly larger than a garage, but its walls were black basalt and its shape suggested the gothic without indulging in it.

Like an archaic family joke, the Martin chapel was dedicated to that joyless ascetic, Saint Jerome. Corra didn't know why her family had chosen him, though she suspected it was his bookish qualities that had drawn her ancestors.

Even though the chapel was abandoned, the engraving over the doorway remained intact: *Quid futurum est esse iam coeperit.*

"Begin now to be what you will be hereafter," Corra said softly, as if it were a prayer itself. She turned to me with a history lesson. "Jerome favored the buried places, when he was young, to see the martyrs' bodies and relics for himself. He felt that seeing those sacred bones would absolve him of his earthly sins."

We went inside, and Corra showed me the door to the Martin tomb and the stairs that led down to the graves. The stone walls leading down were as pocked as the walls of her basement. She asked if I knew of the Fosse Ardeatine, near Rome, near the catacombs Jerome haunted in his youth. I did not then, but I learned.

#

When Corra rested, which became more and more of each day, I went exploring.

I knew there were other people still in town, but I saw only fleeting evidence of them. Holyoke had contracted. I could not see the town as Corra did. I had no memory to fill the gaps.

The main street was a wide stretch of abandoned stores, windows intact, merchandise fading in the weak sun. The municipal building was empty in these strange times, as was the unlocked, partially stocked grocery store, and a church whose denomination escaped me. Here and there I could see the blue flicker of fluorescent lights where, somehow, electricity still flowed.

On the far side of an overgrown park I found the library. It was without power, abandoned as the rest of the town's infrastructure. The doors had blown open in some storm and the vestibule was clotted with mud. But the books had been left mostly alone. The main rooms were bright with the grey light that poured through the large, streaked windows.

I searched through the stacks until I found the books I needed, thick with dampness but intact. I collected layperson's science, paleontology and geology and archeology. I dug out books of folklore and myth. I grabbed a few science journals I thought I would understand.

I lugged my finds back home with me, where the light was constant. I had little else to do but read.

I read all the nonfiction first, answering the questions Corra had raised. And then I dug deeper into folklore and myth, back to the Greeks and their buried gods, and the gods they stole and renamed. It was all there, scattered like fossil bones, fragmentary, incomplete, but clear enough. Clear enough.

The urge to burrow deep into the belly of the earth has been with us as long as we have been human. The Neanderthals who buried their dead a thousand feet deep in the Bruniquel Caves must have felt the tug, and the butchers who stumbled into the Fosse Ardeatine.

But our history is also haunted by the convergence of elemental forces, the earth and the sea. And so the Celts made sacrifices in the ocean-washed caves in the Moray Firth. And divers at the Eagle's Nest drowned in the depths of the earth.

Those places are gone now, lost. But something deep calls us, and always, always, we find a way to answer.

#

The days dragged on. One Gorney or another made sure the generator ran, and that some kind of food was left on the doorstep for us. I walked, and I read. Sometimes I spent time with Corra. I would help her down the stairs and we would walk as far as the chapel. But the damp air weighed her down. She had so little energy left. My company seemed to exhaust her.

As Corra grew weaker, she grew less certain of her family's ways. We stopped our trips to the chapel. She would no longer bear looking down that long stairway into the dark.

She became obsessed with her impending death. She grew demanding, pressing me to promise I would not bring her to her family tomb. She wanted her body burned, and the ashes taken to the high peaks above Holyoke and thrown to the wind. She did not fear dying, not the great swallowing void of not being, not even the relentless pain of the process. She dreaded the thought of being sunk into the earth. She feared what would become of her after.

I promised her anything, to keep her still. There was so little of her left.

#

Soon enough, Corra passed beyond any comfort I could offer. Her skin had been golden once, before fading to its present dull brass. The fever that rode her gave her sunken cheeks a lying flush, lent her eyes a false brightness. But she was wasted into a barely fleshed scarecrow, her arms and legs sticks inside her clothes.

"It's moving in me. Like worms. It hurts," she told me, her voice a ghost. "Go find the Gorneys."

I left her and stepped out into dusk. I took the car, glad the neglected battery still held a charge. I drove until I found the Gorneys' house by the electric light shining through its windows. The front screen door was propped open. I knocked on the doorframe.

Dishes clinked inside the house. Water ran. I heard low voices but could not catch the words. At last an older woman came to the door, trailed by a tall young man.

"Are you Mrs. Gorney?" I asked, suddenly uncertain.

"Anna," she said. "And Anthony."

She showed no surprise at my appearance.

"It's Corra," I said. "She's dying."

Anna Gorney shrugged. "That's why she came home."

I was jarred by her bluntness. "Please. You'll help with the arrangements? She wants her ashes scattered over the sea. Are any funeral homes even still open?"

She looked at me with what might have been pity, or scorn.

"We'll do what we have to," she said. "Go home. We'll come."

"Thank you," I said, and gladly left the Gorneys behind me as I drove back to the house.

I went upstairs, into the comfort of the light. Corra had curled up on her side, her face to the wall, whispering steadily of burning and flight. Her faded voice went on for hours. I sat with her and listened. Her words were a jumble, noise without sense. Eventually she stopped speaking at all, and very late that night she died, gasping from the pain.

#

The next morning, the Gorneys appeared on the doorstep. Their knocking broke the spell of silence that held the Martin house. I let them in.

"She's dead," I said by way of greeting.

"Yes. I know," Anna said. She and her son brushed past me and went up to Corra. I stayed downstairs. They knew what they were doing. I didn't question how they knew.

They came down after a short while, with the long bony length of Corra's corpse carried over their shoulders. Her body was wrapped in a grey cloth as fine as spiderweb, and so clingy I could see the hollows of her eyes. Anna must have had the cloth in her bag. There was nothing like that in the house.

"She can't go down yet," Anna said. "We have to make things ready for her."

I roused. "She wanted to be cremated. She doesn't want to be put in the ground."

Anna stared at me, her eyes hard.

"They all say it. Her mother said the same thing, and her grandmother too. I've tended them all at the end."

"Oh," I said.

Anthony stood quietly behind his mother.

"People get scared when they're dying. But she knew what she really wanted. It's her responsibility. It's why she came home."

"Oh, but," I said, and stopped. I wanted to follow Corra's wishes, and I wanted her to be safe with her ancestors, away from this strange, decayed world. I wanted to not be caught here, without her. I didn't yet understand. The machinery moved on without me.

"We'll leave her in the parlor until it's done," Anna said.

I nodded, tired, not willing to argue. Corra was dead, and it didn't matter. I did not think it through.

They lay Corra on the long couch facing the blank television. From another hidden pocket, Anna unfurled another long length of fabric, this one spangled in silver, and draped it over my wife's dead form. She bent to smooth it, and I saw her move her hands in a way that suggested the sign of the cross. But it was not a cross she drew there over Corra's quiet heart.

Anna straightened and looked at her work, then nodded to me. "Come, Anthony," she said to her son. And they left me alone.

I spent the night in the parlor with Corra, glad of the electric lights that cast back the shadows. Nothing moved in the house. The only sound was the thrum of the generator below. Even so, I imagined my wife might still be breathing inside her shroud. I thought I heard a soft, wet motion. I thought I saw something slide beneath the wrappings, working them loose. But the faint exhalations were only the beginnings of decomposition, relentless even in the cool night. I moved my chair back from her, and eventually fell asleep. I dreamed of Corra, on a pyre that would not kindle.

#

Anna Gorney did not come back to the house for two days. She and her son had opened up the Martin tomb and cleared the neglected passageway to its end, and then dug a new niche into the soft, honeycombed stone for Corra's swaddled remains.

By now Corra had begun to stink plainly of decay. A thin, vile liquid stained the fine cloth of her shroud. But Anna Gorney and her son did not flinch away from lifting her again to carry her to the chapel. They walked at a stately pace and let me trail behind them. I could hear them whispering roughly to each other. It might have been a conversation, it might have been a song. I did not listen closely enough to tell.

Instead I wandered along and gathered an armload of lilies from the untended gardens along the way, carrying the blooms instead of helping to bear my wife. When we reached the chapel, I had to crush the lilies against my chest to open the door for the Gorneys. They passed me with their burden, and for a moment I was truly left outside of it, outside the chapel, outside the ritual, outside the cloistered history of my wife and the town.

Overwhelmed, I followed them in. They had already descended the steps to the tomb, and I hurried down to see them set my Corra in her place.

The heady smell of the lilies was cloying in the narrow confines of the grave, but not strong enough to mask the rot. I lay the bright flowers at Corra's feet and tried not to breathe too deeply. I wondered how guilty I should be, that I hadn't insisted on burning her. I looked for the Gorneys, but they had gone up, leaving me to whatever rites I would do. But I did nothing. I could not believe my Corra had been reduced to this.

And yet, I still suffered the niggling doubt that she was not truly gone. The words carved over the chapel's door fed my imagination. Begin now to be what you will be hereafter—but when does *now* begin?

#

Every day I went to visit her, a lone pilgrim in an empty town. The Gorneys kept to themselves, their duties fulfilled. If anyone else still called this town home, they kept to themselves as well. I saw no one. Just as well; I did not need the pressure of contact.

Every day I let myself into the chapel and descended to her. Every day the distance seemed a few yards longer, the slant of the floor steeper, the air warmer and strangely flavoured with salt. Every day I brought her fresh flowers from the gardens running to seed, lilies, roses, phlox, all sweet and suffocating in the close stone channel but never fragrant enough. Her silvery shroud grew dark with stains as she withered inside it. I marked how she changed, how the clinging wet fabric revealed a new form inside the old. She had been my wife. As long as she remained in the riddled stone crypt where her family was, she would be.

I entertained wild thoughts built on myths, of magically bringing her back. Of her wanting to come back. Of her loving me enough to make her way out of that consuming darkness.

Every day I walked slowly down the long spiral, to Corra, my Eurydice, to tempt her back into the air. But I am not Orpheus. I could not persuade her to follow me even a little way back.

#

Today, after two weeks of invariable routine, I needed to change. I left the house and gathered what weedy flowers still bloomed, but I did not turn immediately toward Corra's familiar tomb. The day was cool and grey, with a wet breeze coming off the cooling ocean. Summer was reaching its inevitable end.

I walked into the wind, toward the edge of town where the land fell away into the sea below. Scrub grass gave way to bare pitted rock. The wind became a force on the cliff's edge, blowing my hair back. I looked for gulls, but there were none to see.

The ocean below was as milky as jade, its shush and rumble masked by the wind streaming past my ears. I felt smothered in the sound of it, separated from what was left of the rest of the world.

I finally turned my head away from the wind's direct path, and could finally hear the sea. But there was no human sound, no bird cry, no noise of something alive. The air moved. The sea churned. And the sky hung like dull silk above it all, rippled and weighted by something behind it.

I had never realized how alone I was before that moment. Not just from Corra's death. From the world's.

Nothing, in the end, is sacrosanct. We die. Traditions are misremembered or forgotten. There is no way to stop it happening, with lives as brief as ours. There are gods we shall never see, because we no longer remember how.

I threw my handful of flowers into the sea. They scattered and drifted in the wind, tumbling down the cliff face before falling bruised upon the water. It didn't matter. It meant nothing to me once it was done. I was no part of this town. I didn't belong here, to this tradition. Not with Corra gone. I didn't belong to her either. Not anymore. I watched the waves swallow the flowers down.

And then the sky ripped open, the grey fabric of it shredded by profound light, and in an instant the roar of thunder followed. The smooth clouds flexed into stormy masses, muscular as a cat.

I cringed. Mine is not the only memory.

With the first slap of rain an attention bore down on me, the attention of something that had no measure of its own strength and no concern for mine. I fled from the wind and the terrible sky, driven back into town by the storm.

#

The muddy streets of Holyoke were empty but for me. The rain stung like splinters and the wind was a lash. I should have run back up the hill to the house, but the sky knew where I was. The chapel was closer.

I wrestled open the door beneath the inscription and escaped the swarming rain. Saint Jerome's words were no longer any comfort or hope. Even beneath the stone roof I felt exposed.

As I wiped water from my face, I realized that someone sat on the step to the altar. My skin tingled as the hair on my arms lifted in fear. In the foggy grey light the person seemed misshapen and blurred, human only by suggestion. Then lightning flashed and the figure stood up, coalescing into Anthony Gorney.

"What are you doing here?" I said before I could stop myself.

He shrugged. I realized I had never heard him speak.

Then Gorney opened the door to the tomb for me, and gestured that I should go down. Lightning crackled, lighting the passage and first few steps with blue radiance. It seemed as if the light flowed down the worn stone, seeped into the cracks, and was absorbed by the darkness.

Gorney gestured again.

"All right," I said. "I've been here every day. Of course I'm going down."

I reached into my pocket for the flashlight I carried, glad I had put in fresh batteries. Gorney did not move aside as I passed, forcing me closer to him than I ever wanted to be. He smelled of old, wet things, like mold on cloth. I didn't look at him, but I heard his rough breathing in my ear as I stepped down.

I passed the first turn in the stairs when fear closed my throat. The long winding tunnel smelled of earth and salt. The myths I had read swarmed in my imagination.

Before I could turn back I heard the door slam shut, the key grind in the lock, the retreat of footsteps across the chapel floor.

"Gorney!" I yelled, but I was ignored. I heard the outer door to the chapel bang closed. Then I heard only the dim, distant rhythm of rain on the high chapel roof.

I was sealed in with my wife, and all her kin.

My flashlight cut the dark, drawing out the shadows. I did not bother to try the door behind me. I had opened it enough times to know its weight and its well-oiled machinery. I went down, as I was meant to.

The corridor ran on longer than I remembered from all my previous visits. As I went deeper it was not the reek of the grave but the rank stench of the sea that laded the air. I passed the dozens of niches I always counted on my way to Corra, each with its pile of dust. This time it struck me that the names over them, all the names I could read, were female.

The tomb spiraled down and down, screwed into the earth. I had a sense of the corridor turning on itself, like a Möbius ring, like Oroboros. At times it seemed as if I were climbing, but gravity pulled strangely at me and I had to fight against it to move on. At other times a step would bring a sickening lurch like the drop of an elevator, but the rock remained firm beneath my feet.

The sides of the corridor glistened, dank with seeping water, and the air grew increasingly hot.

When I finally reached the end of the corridor, I expected to see the shadow of my Corra in her ragged shroud, as slumped and empty as I had left her yesterday. But she was gone, her niche vacant. I cast my light around, looking for signs of some terrible prank. Dropped in the dust was her dismembered hand, half-open, cupping nothing, the skin tight and pulling the bones together. The index finger extended in a weak curve to point further down the now-elongated corridor, deeper into the dark.

She was down there, moving in the earth. I knew it.

#

I followed her direction. The tunnel continued as far as my light would show it.

There were no more niches, just pitted, black rock walls. It is the same rock as the chapel, and the intrusion in her basement. It is the same rock that underlies the deep sea itself, born there at the rifts in great molten upwellings that flow slowly away to reshape the rest of the world in their time.

These black walls should have been smooth and solid, the roots of the world. But they were as pocked as limestone. The corridor rustled with the sound of sand on sand. I blamed my own footsteps. The smell of salt here made me choke. I cannot imagine how far down I have travelled.

#

And then I realized that my flashlight was not the only source of light in the depths. Ahead of me I could just discern a pale, bioluminescent glow spilling up from an even deeper place.

The floor sloped down gently. I stepped down into the light.

Corra sat in state in the grotto that opened before me, a damp velvet cushion beneath her, her shoulders draped in silver cloth. Fungal things bloomed around her in a strange bounty, waving delicate yellow filaments in the bloodwarm, still air.

Her bones had been stripped of all soft flesh, and polished until they shone like pearl. I saw with some surprise how narrow and shallow her jaw was, how wide set her eyes. Her bones had changed down here, or living flesh had hidden these deformities. Now they were bare, a truth revealed.

But her eyes—the sockets were not empty after all. Like a heavy tide, a luminous jelly rolled up to fill them, shimmered and focused and saw me. For too long I could only meet that alien gaze, struck dumb by the spark and fade of those viscous depths. It was like looking into the night sky, or deep water. And then, she recognized me.

The tendons that held her bent jaw to her skull creaked and slithered as she opened her mouth. A hiss of a voice slipped out. The moist grating sound grew louder all around, and slippery vermin came from every crack that could hide them. One slithered over my shoe and clung to the leg of my pants before I shouted in gross fear and kicked it away. It was a pale grey thing, limber and slick and primitive, one of the things that scraped through the rock, making passage for what still would come.

The myths and folklore have lost so much in translation. The raw edges of our need for burial have been rubbed to dullness by time.

There are elemental places that demand to be opened and then appeased. Like other caves, like other catacombs, the Martin tomb was one. The Martins opened it willingly and answered the call with their own blood. There were benefits to their sacrifice.

Beside my Corra is an empty throne carved out of the grotto itself, black and ancient stone worn smooth by countless grey bodies sliding across it, decorated with a lattice of crumbling bones. The seat is too high for a human, too angled, too deep.

Even further beneath us I can hear a huge, even, booming sound, like an ancient bell, like waves against a hollow rock wall. The constant slithering of the grey things stops. They retreat into their many, many holes.

Corra is not my Eurydice. No. She is Persephone, queen in the dark. And I am not her king.

Publication History

Fracture *first appeared in Unnerving Magazine: Issue #3, July 2017*

The Bones *first appeared in Weirdbook # 41, June 2019*

Pretty in the Dark *first appeared in Test Patterns: Creature Features, Planet X Publications, October 2018*

Fallen *original to this publication*

Here Is Where Your Proud Waves Halt *first appeared in Weirdbook Annual #1: Witches, October 2017*

Signals *first appeared in Galileo's Theme Park, Third Flatiron Publishing, June 2018*

One Last Mile *first appeared in Twice-Told: A Collection of Doubles, Cthonic Matter, February 2019*

Imago *first appeared in Bracken issue II, August 2016*

A Clockwork Muse *first appeared in Weirdbook # 31, September 2015*

In the Bright Sunlight *first appeared in Turn to Ash, Vol. 3, December 2017*

Downstream *first appeared in New Myths, December 2016*

Underneath *first appeared in Green Inferno: The World Celebrates Your Demise, Tenebrous Press, July 2021*

Serpentine *original to this publication*

Chrysalis *original to this publication*

Antinomia *first appeared in Cthulhusattva, Martian Migraine Press, 2016*

Afterimage *original to this publication*

Summer's End *a version appeared in What October Brings: A Lovecraftian Celebration of Halloween, Celano Press, October 2018*

Strange Bodies *first appeared in Mythic # 6, April 2018*

Still *first appeared in Mythic # 14, October 2020*

Winterking *first appeared in Alien Abduction, Robot Cowgirl Publishing, 2015*

The Grave of Angels *first appeared in Vastarien Volume 4 Issue 1, June 2021*

About the Author

ERICA RUPPERT, HWA, SFWA. lives in northern New Jersey with her husband and too many cats. Her first novella, *Sisters in Arms*, was released by Trepidatio Publishing in 2021; her second, *To the Shore, to the Sea*, was released by Hiraeth Publishing in February 2023. Her short stories have appeared in magazines including *Vastarien*, *LampLight*, and *Nightmare*, on podcasts including PodCastle, and in multiple anthologies. When she is not writing, she runs, bakes, and gardens with more enthusiasm than skill.

JUL 1 9 2023